COCHRANE

- - JUL 2018

D0896361

DEATH BY DINOSAUR

A SAM STELLAR MYSTERY

DEATH BY DINOSAUR

A SAM STELLAR MYSTERY

JACQUELINE GUEST

COTEAU BOOKS

© Jacqueline Guest, 2018

All rights reserved. No part of this publication may be reproduced, stored in a retrieval system, or transmitted, in any form or by any means, without the prior written consent of the publisher or a licence from The Canadian Copyright Licensing Agency (Access Copyright). For an Access Copyright licence, visit www.accesscopyright.ca or call toll-free to 1-800-893-5777.

In this book, names, characters, places, and incidents either are the product of the author's imagination or are used fictitiously. Any resemblance to actual persons, living or dead, is coincidental.

Edited by Kathryn Cole
Designed by Jamie Olson
Photographs courtesy of the Royal Tyrrell Museum, Drumheller, Canada
Printed and bound in Canada

Library and Archives Canada Cataloguing in Publication

Guest, Jacqueline, author
      Death by dinosaur : a Sam Stellar mystery / Jacqueline Guest.

Issued in print and electronic formats.
ISBN 978-1-55050-943-4 (softcover).--ISBN 978-1-55050-944-1
(PDF).--ISBN 978-1-55050-945-8 (HTML).--ISBN 978-1-55050-946-5 (Kindle)
      I. Title.

PS8563.U365D43 2018   jC813'.54   C2017-907477-6
                                   C2017-907478-4

Library of Congress Control Number: 2017962855

2517 Victoria Avenue
Regina, Saskatchewan
Canada S4P 0T2
www.coteaubooks.com

Available in Canada from:
Publishers Group Canada
2440 Viking Way
Richmond, British Columbia
Canada V6V 1N2

10 9 8 7 6 5 4 3 2 1

Coteau Books gratefully acknowledges the financial support of its publishing program by: the Saskatchewan Arts Board, The Canada Council for the Arts, the Government of Saskatchewan through Creative Saskatchewan, the City of Regina. We further acknowledge the [financial] support of the Government of Canada. Nous reconnaissons l'appui [financier] du gouvernement du Canada.

For Mary – forever friends
from alpha to omega

Chapter 1

NEW CASE

GUARD MURDERED IN DINOSAUR BONE THEFT!
Police Baffled

Samantha Stellar couldn't tear her eyes away from the newspaper article. The headline screamed for attention, especially the 'police baffled' part. It was all there in black and white – an unexplained, unsolved theft with a deadly twist. She pushed her glasses back up onto the bridge of her nose and smiled. It was exactly what an aspiring spy such as herself dreamed of – a mystery suitable for James Bond, code name 007.

Sam nudged her cousin, Paige Carlson, who was sleeping in the seat beside her. "Wake up."

"What? Are we finally there?" Paige mumbled groggily.

"Nope, still rollin' across the Alberta prairie in our trusty Greyhound. But, on a cooler subject, did you know that a couple of months ago there was a South American dinosaur fossil stolen from a museum in Ontario? During the theft a guard was killed with the fossilized horn from a *Triceratops*. Can you believe it? It's the mysterious case of…da-da-da-dum: *Death by Dinosaur*." She used her best theatrical voice for drama on the last part.

Sam could imagine the gruesome scene the police had found. The dead body, its sightless eyes staring into infinity, the massive horn protruding from the hapless victim's back. Or front, the article hadn't said. And blood! She was sure there'd been enough to keep any Count from Transylvania positively gorged.

"That's messed up!" Paige said sympathetically. "Truly a brutal way to go. What I don't get is why you woke me up to give me this really, *really* old news flash."

Sam heard the irritation in her cousin's voice but went on anyway. "It wasn't the only theft. The string of targets stretches right across Canada into every museum with so much as a chunk of coprolite. That's fossilized dino dung in case you aren't up on all things Jurassic. Of course, I've been tracking these dinosaur bone heists from the beginning and have information from every web page, blog, twitter and tweet."

"Yeah, so, what does any of this have to do with us?"

Paige had gone from irritated to confused, and Sam knew she had only seconds before she lost her cousin completely. "Connect the dots, Paige. Dinosaur bones are being stolen. Every dino museum in Canada *except one* has been hit. And where are we going to work this summer?"

Her cousin blinked, not connecting a single dot. "Um, don't tell me...the Tyrrell Museum of Thingamabob."

"It's the Royal Tyrrell Museum of Palaeontology and it's filled with dinosaur bits and bones. It`s also the only one *not* on the hit list. You know what this means?" Sam tried to keep the excitement out of her voice.

"Uh...our museum isn't as popular with murdering thieves as the others?"

Sam ignored her cousin's comment. "It means the Tyrrell will probably be next. This museum is a huge deal in the Dino 'Verse, and it doesn't make sense to skip it."

"So why have they?" Paige pushed herself semi-upright in the sagging seat.

Sam thought about this. "That, cousin, is a very good question. Maybe the crooks are working their way down some kind of heist list and the Tyrrell is last. You know, kind of like keeping dessert as a reward for eating your Brussels sprouts. It's a good thing we're going to be there."

This got Paige's attention. "What aren't you telling me and what are you plotting? Samantha Stellar, have you conned me into being on this bus to Drumheller with you?"

Sam ignored her cousin's rather accurate accusation. "It all started when my *weirdometer* went off. Remember I told you about the odd feeling I get when I'm onto something important? Well, when I saw the first article on the museum thefts I got a particularly high reading."

Paige scowled. "Don't start with the hocus-pocus stuff, Sam. And you still haven't told me what any of this has to do with us."

"You are *so-o-o-o* suspicious. All I meant was, you know, *if* the Tyrrell were to acquire, say, an exotic South American dinosaur fossil, things could get exciting."

"*Fine,*" Paige said, managing to work a big helping of suspicion into this word too. "As long as you're not conjuring up some government conspiracy fantasy." She pulled a small hot-pink mirror out of her purse and scrutinized her face. "*Crap on a cracker!* I drooled in my sleep and washed away my perfect pout." She hastily repaired her smudged makeup then shook her bright-red hair back into perfect curls that framed her heart-shaped face.

Sam's cousin was the "early bloomer" in the family. She was all glam – tall, slim and with killer cheekbones.

Sam, on the other hand, was what you called "healthy." She was on the short side and her body type screamed "athlete" with muscles that went way past toned and no hint of curves. Add to this pencil-straight auburn hair and campfire-smoke grey eyes behind black-framed glasses and you clearly had a girl who'd never willingly be on a fashion shoot. She was happy with the way she looked and didn't bother with makeup, even when there was a new hot "student body" at school.

As Sam watched her cousin's *toilette,* she decided not to add how she'd kept up with all things Tyrrell, and if what she'd read was correct, she was sure this museum would be targeted next. A perfect case for *Sam Stellar, Super Sleuth!* (She'd decided this was the title she'd have on her business cards when she actually had…well…a business.)

This carefully collected intel meant she needed to be behind the scenes at the famous palaeontology centre in order to foil the upcoming crime.

Actually, being on-site when the thieves struck had presented a real challenge. Then – a miraculous sign from the heavens! Sam's school counsellor told her about the Summer Studies and Work Experience program.

The program was available to students who wanted to learn about a profession they were interested in. As an added bonus, the lucky ones chosen earned extra school credits while doing it. Sam had needed to bring her marks up to get in, which meant studying harder than she ever had in all of her fourteen years on this particular planet, and it had paid off big time.

Convincing her family she was thinking of being a palaeontologist had been the tricky part. Her unexpected career choice was news to them, but when she persuaded Paige (a girl with a rep for being down-to-earth) to sign on, the deal was clinched.

Sam thoughtfully tapped the article she was holding, then decided to tell her cousin everything she had deduced. "Paige, I've got a hunch we won't have to wait long for the next theft." She pulled another clipping out of her backpack and held it up with a flourish. "Read this."

Finally happy with her appearance, Paige dropped the mirror back into her bag and then read out loud. "*Royal Tyrrell To Receive Unique Colombian Dinosaur Find.* Yeah, so what?"

"Last time I played Where's Waldo, Colombia was in South America. Refer back to previous article." She waved the other piece of newspaper, Chinese fan style. "It's as though the Tyrrell is supplying the perps with mighty tasty bait."

"*Perps?*" Paige cocked one perfect brow at Sam.

"You know – the dirty rats, the low life, the *perpetrators*..." Sam enthusiastically wiggled both her eyebrows at her cousin.

Their discussion was interrupted by a raised voice from the row behind theirs.

"Mom, I had to slug him," a young boy whined. "He hit me first!"

"I don't care who started it. You and your brother are both in trouble, so knock it off." The harried mother was obviously in no mood for scrappy kids. "Excuse me sir," she said in a calm controlled voice adults reserved for other adults, "could you tell me the time?"

"*Si, señora,* it is nearly six o'clock," a man with a strong Spanish accent answered.

Sam froze. Had she heard right?

A Spanish-speaking man on the bus to Drumheller where the Tyrrell Museum with its soon-to-arrive, South-American dinosaur was located! What were the odds?

Sam tingled with an electric buzz and knew her weirdometer had jumped off the scale. Was it only some cosmic coincidence, or had her first case just begun?

"Paige, give me your mirror," she whispered urgently.

"You really should get your own beauty gear." Her exasperated tone said this was covering old ground. "Oh wait, you don't do the fashionista thing, do you? Instead, you borrow mine..." Grumbling, Paige rummaged in her over-over-sized bag, then handed Samantha the small compact.

As casually as possible, Sam held the mirror up as she scoped out the mysterious passenger. She spotted him immediately. The dark suit he wore made him very conspicuous. Everyone else sported denim jeans and ball caps. She committed his details to memory: thin black moustache, dark wavy hair, swarthy complexion. Check, check and *check!* Very Latin, very suspicious!

In case anyone was watching, Sam smudged her mouth

with her finger as though applying lip gloss. She angled the small mirror a little higher and was able to sneak another furtive peek at the man.

That was when Sam saw the conspicuous bulge in his jacket. She gasped, and her heart sped up a beat, or maybe two.

Unless she missed her guess, this dark stranger had a gun hidden under his coat. And in an instant, he became more than mysterious; he became menacing.

Chapter 2

CLUE NúMERO UNO

As the kilometres rolled by, Sam decided surveillance on a bus was pretty easy (where could the guy hide anyway?), which made it simple for her to keep a covert eye on the dark stranger. She continued periodical observations of her suspect; unfortunately, he did nothing to warrant her super-spy attention.

Finally, as twilight faded into dusk, the bus started a steep descent into a lush, green river valley, and the town of Drumheller came into view. It was in this valley that a wonderful treasure trove of dinosaur bones had been found, and because of these finds, the Royal Tyrrell Museum had been built. Along with being an amazing museum, it was an important research facility with top scientists from all over the globe working on fossils.

Even if it hadn't been the next logical target for the thieves, Sam couldn't help being excited about working at the museum. One-hundred-million-year-old bones of the biggest creatures that ever roamed the earth! Truly mind boggling. Maybe she *would* take up dinosaur hunting, between cases.

Turning to take a last peek at her suspect, Sam's attention was unexpectedly grabbed by a young man watching her. The cute blond winked. She spun around feeling her face burn.

He obviously thought she'd been looking at him. Groaning, Sam shrank down into her seat. As soon as she got home, she'd log on to her favourite online academy, The Superior School for Spies, and repeat the class on Undercover Observation Techniques.

◎

After a rather bumpy stop, the passengers gathered their belongings and shuffled down the aisle. Sam waited for her suspect, and then, as he moved past, she stood and accidentally brushed against him.

She was right! There was no mistaking the feel of a semiautomatic in a shoulder holster. "'Scuse me," she mumbled, ducking her head as she reached down for her backpack. She watched him out of the corner of her eye as he continued moving with the other passengers.

Sam followed at a discreet distance, which on a crowded rural bus meant two farmers and a cowboy behind her target. Her cunning master plan: trail her suspect and see what he was up to.

Emerging from the bus, Sam winced as her cousin abruptly changed the master plan.

"Yo! Sam, over here!" Paige yelled in her best hockey-rink voice. "I'm almost positive I put tags on all four of my suitcases but one bag seems to be missing. Can you help find it?"

Samantha inspected the tidy row of suitcases on the sidewalk and had to admit, they were all very similar. Finding Paige's was like picking one suspect out of a lineup of clones. Her own battered neon-green bag was easy to find and she pulled it out of the row then added it to Paige's pile. "Doesn't the driver deliver these to the *inside* of the building?"

"Apparently not in the *très chic* town of Drumheller," Paige said, trying not to bend over too far in her tiny red-and-black plaid skirt as she continued reading the name tags. "This is stupid dumb! Does everyone in the world have exactly the same black suitcase as me? For crying out loud, Sam, help me before I'm arrested for indecent exposure!" She tugged at her skirt.

Sam was about to mention she had her own stuff to worry about when she glimpsed her suspicious suspect disappearing into the terminal. As any covert agent knows, when tailing someone, timing was crucial. She grabbed the two random bags nearest her. "I'll take these inside for you, Paige." And before her cousin could yell at her, Sam hurried toward the doors.

Once inside, Sam quickly scanned the room. No sign of him. *"Rotten rodents!"* she cursed. This was not an auspicious start to her spying career.

Abandoning the suitcases, Sam searched for a pay phone to call her mother's long-time friend, Mrs. O'Reilly, who ran the boarding house where they'd be staying. Inconveniently, Sam didn't have a cellphone, and that was a constant source of argument at home. Her parents thought the ability to Snapchat, text or *#anything* to her friends 24/7 was unnecessary. They simply didn't understand modern social networking!

The fact she'd lost her new cell two days after she'd received it as a Christmas present might have had something to do with her parents' negative take on the situation. It had fallen out of her pocket while she'd been skiing in the back country and was probably frozen in a glacier by now.

Paige was no help. Her supersize cell with its sparkling pink rhinestone case was fabulous, but as she continually forgot to charge the battery, it was more of a pretty paperweight than a functioning phone.

Finding a public pay phone was a bit of a treasure hunt. There weren't many around and the ones that still existed were always tucked into some hidden alcove, invisible to mortals.

Fortunately, in a bus terminal the size of a broom closet, there weren't many places to stash the booth. Across the room, Sam saw the only communications kiosk in the depot – and it was being used.

She caught her breath. The tall guy in the red phone booth, which could have been straight off the streets of old London, was her mystery man!

Her cousin, now dragging her complete set of all four

over- packed suitcases, came to a halt behind Sam.

"Paige, do you see the guy using the phone?" Sam asked urgently.

Sam's cousin scrutinized the man in the booth. "Yeah, why? He's not only too old for you," she wrinkled her small nose, "he's not yummy at all."

"He's the suspicious man from the bus! The one I've been watching. Check him out – he's writing something down."

"What suspicious man? Why were you watching him?" Paige's mouth drew into a hard line. "Oh, no you don't. No way, Sam! You're not going to start with that secret agent stuff, are you? Every time we go anywhere, you turn it into a James Bond movie. It's just some old geezer, for crying out loud! He probably runs the local hardware store and was in Calgary ordering new toilet seats for outhouses."

She pulled hard on one of her wheeled suitcases, sending it smack into Sam's heel. "You promised me on this gig there would be all kinds of cute, scientific-type guys back from months of working on lonely digs, or hanging out in boring labs and in need of stimulating conversation from a stunning young woman...such as myself. That homey is none of the above."

Wincing, Sam bent to rub her bruised foot. "Do you have a driver's license for your wheeled weapon?" As she watched, the dark-haired man stepped out of the phone booth and started across the terminal. "Duck!" She reached up and pulled Paige's arm down. The rest of her cousin's body obediently followed.

"*Sa-man-tha...*" Paige warned, carefully pronouncing each syllable. "I mean it. No nutty cloak-and-dagger stuff. We're almost fifteen now, you know – *practising adults*. We don't have time for your superspy scenarios."

"*Pa-i-ge,*" Sam reciprocated with the three-syllable pronunciation, which was hard to do with a one-syllable name. "He's dangerous." She knew this was going to be a tough sell. "When he was leaving the bus, I bumped into him and felt a concealed weapon."

"You actually *saw* this alleged concealed weapon?" Paige's tone had *doubtful* written large.

"No, Sherlock," Sam said impatiently. "It was *concealed*. But it felt exactly like a gun."

"Or a hairbrush, or a lumpy wallet, or keys, or who knows what! Your *imagination* says it was a gun." Paige dismissed the idea with a flick of her hand.

Sam shook her head. "Sceptic! I know that guy couldn't tell a Robertson screw driver from a Stillson wrench."

She sprinted for the pay phone and had nearly made it when she intercepted an elderly woman heading for the same unoccupied booth. "Excuse me." Sam pushed in front of the flustered senior. "Telephone sanitation officer!" Flashing her library card, she slammed the door shut.

The irate woman beat on the booth with her cane. Paige glared in Sam's direction, then stalked off, suitcases trailing behind.

"Great!" Sam grumbled. "So much for backup."

Ignoring the loud banging, Sam inspected the booth. Everything was normal. No secret messages taped to the bottom of the phone or code words etched into the glass. She noticed the ancient directory had been left lying open. Tipping the page slightly, she could make out a faint impression. With her trusty yellow Ticonderoga pencil from her backpack, she carefully shaded over the ghost message. *Museo 403-555-4157* appeared.

Tearing off a small corner of the page, Sam quickly jotted the name and number down, then held up one finger to let the woman know she was nearly through. Fishing in her blue jeans for change, Sam thumbed the coins into the phone and dialled Mrs. O'Reilly to arrange transportation.

The thumping became a lot more energetic. For an old girl, this lady had quite a swing. Smiling sweetly, Sam surrendered the pay phone before any security personnel showed up.

Excitement built as she hurried after her cousin and held up the paper. "Well...?"

Paige frowned at the crumpled scrap. "So...it's obviously Mr. Museo's phone number. There's nothing clandestine about writing down a phone number – besides, you don't know Mr. X wrote it."

Sam scoffed, "Mr. X? You're not serious? That's way too cliché for our mystery man." She thought about the perfect tag for her prime suspect; then the corners of her mouth crooked up. "Me, I think it should be Agent D, for Double-O-Dino. Plus, it's a darn good thing our country's security isn't in your hands, Ms Carlson. This is practically oozing with intrigue. I saw him write something and I'm sure this *Museo* guy's phone number is it."

The woman in the booth was still shaking her fist in their direction and giving her opinion in a way that made Sam wish she couldn't lip-read quite so well. A sailor could take lessons from her. Obviously, that particular phone was off limits and Sam made a mental note to call Mr. Museo on the first free land line she found outside the terminal. She simply had to get another cellphone. She felt like she was on her own lonely planet without one.

While they stood in front of the depot waiting for their ride, Sam saw another passenger from the bus, the blond dude. Cringing at the memory of being busted spying, she tried to make herself as inconspicuous as possible by crouching behind Paige's mountain of suitcases. Her own bag was too small and too 'look-at-me' green.

"What are you doing?" her cousin asked curiously.

Sam motioned Paige to be quiet – annoyingly her cousin didn't decode her frantic signals and continued loudly.

"Sam! Did you drop something? Get up. I'll help you look. Got a cramp in your leg? Those are killers. Rub your calf –"

"Paige – *be quiet!*" Sam hissed. "I haven't dropped any-thing. I don't want to be seen!"

"By whom?" Paige stood on tiptoe, rubbernecking left, then right. "Oh, my, Miss Scarlet! Is it your many fans hounding you for your autograph again? Perhaps the *paparazzi* found out you were coming and they're trying to get a money shot."

"Will you *puh-lease* keep your voice down!" Sam peered over the pile of suitcases. The hot guy was nowhere to be seen. "Okay, it's safe."

Her cousin's lips formed a perfect *O*. "*O-o-o-o!* That's really comforting to know. I thought we were both done for!"

Sam stood and dusted off her jeans. "Civilians. *Humph!*"

Chapter 3

NUMBER REVEALED

Mrs. O'Reilly, a silver-haired woman of enormous girth, called Sam and Paige to breakfast early the next morning. Entering the dining room, she clapped to get the attention of the other boarders seated at the large, round wooden table. "Ladies and gentlemen, these two young ladies are Samantha Stellar and Paige Carlson. They'll be staying with us for the summer while they're working at the museum." She seated herself and motioned for the girls to do the same.

Smiling, Sam nodded at the other guests. Unexpectedly, her gaze locked with a pair of ice-blue eyes.

"We meet again, as they say in the movies." The blond guy from the bus winked at her mischievously. "My name's Jackson Lunde."

Sam tried and failed to be cool. "Uh, hi," she replied weakly, wishing she had a cloak of invisibility. Making a fool of herself to a stranger on a bus was one thing, bumping into him at the breakfast table was something else.

Her cousin was not as shy. "Hey, I'm Paige." She scooted around the table to sit beside him. "You seem familiar. Have we met?"

Sam sank into the chair in front of her, avoiding any more conversation.

"Actually, you might have seen me on the bus from Calgary yesterday. I was coming back from the university."

Sam didn't say a word. She was wearing teal-coloured skinny jeans and a striped top to match and now concentrated very hard on picking an imaginary piece of lint off the jeans.

"University, huh? How fascinating!" Paige gushed as she settled in for a long chat. "What are you studying?"

Sam wished she were sitting closer so she could kick her nosy cousin under the table.

"With a little luck and a lot of hard work I hope to be a geologist." Jackson passed Paige a plate of maple sausages. "Then I want to specialize in palaeontology. I guess I'll be seeing a lot more of you two since, for a while anyway, I'm also working at the museum."

Sam busied herself with her breakfast.

"What a coincidence, Jack – you don't mind if I call you *Jack*, do you?" Paige asked coquettishly. "I'm planning on a career in palaeontology myself! Perhaps you could give me some pointers on how to get started." She reached for the eggs. "Sam's not planning on any sort of normal job. She's had her heart set on being a secret agent since she was seven."

As every head at the table turned toward her, Sam wished the floor would open up and swallow her whole, or at least take a big bite out of her talkative cousin. She cleared her throat noisily. "Actually, despite my family's *non*-support," she stared pointedly at Paige, "I do think it would be interesting to work for the Canadian Security Intelligence Service, commonly known as CSIS." Sam didn't mention all her friends thought she was cracked too. She had to admit it was an odd choice of occupation, but ever since elementary school she'd wanted to be in the spy game. She'd stuck to her dream and now she was ready to solve her first real mystery.

"Sounds intriguing," said the white-haired gentleman sitting next to Sam. "My name's Danny Flannigan, and I hope your stay will be a pleasant one. And as for your choice of a career, it is a mite unusual. But remember what a fella named Thoreau said: 'If a man does not keep pace with his companion, perhaps it is because he hears a different drummer. Let him step to the music he hears, however measured or far away.'"

Sam's embarrassment eased a little. It was nice to think she was right, even if she wasn't being the same as everyone else. "Thanks, Mr. Flannigan. Do you work at the museum also?"

"Heavens, no!" he chuckled. "You might say I'm between bookings. I'm an entertainer, a comedian, in fact. However, since my agent hasn't called in some years now, I mostly help Marie around the boarding house." Mrs. O'Reilly blushed, lowering her lashes demurely. "And the name's Danny, not Mr. Flannigan."

"I'm Rose Hocking," a pretty woman with curly brown hair and a peculiar accent said as she introduced herself. "I work at an importing company that deals a lot with the museum. By the way," she added, "the accent is Welsh, not English."

"And she'll never let you forget it!" The man sitting next to her laughed. "I'm John Cooper. I hope you ladies will visit me at the bank."

Sam saw his fingers were long and fine-boned, more suited to a concert pianist than a guy who counts loonies and toonies all day.

"Are you the prez in charge of the loot?" Paige joked, then quickly corrected herself when Sam sent her the evil eye. "I mean, what do you do at the bank, John?"

"Not the president quite yet," he laughed. "Actually, I'm the only male teller in all of Drumheller."

"Gottcha. Starting at the bottom, huh?" Paige said sagely.

John was taken aback at this. "There's nothing wrong with being a teller. I enjoy my job."

Paige realized she'd insulted John and she began to eat vigorously, ending any more conversation.

Sam felt much better. Seeing Paige with her size nines in her mouth was cosmic justice. Until now, Sam had been the only one holding a crazy-teenager card.

Danny went on with the introductions. "And I've kept the best for last, the LaSalle sisters, Clarisse and Abigail. They're movie stars, at least Clarisse is. She was a child star back in the late fifties, before movies were ninety per cent special effects. Abigail is her agent. Isn't that right, ladies?"

The two fragile ladies agreed demurely. They reminded Sam of a pair of delicate porcelain dolls you'd see in an antique store window.

While everyone was busy eating, Sam thought it was a good opportunity to slip away and call her parents to let them know they had arrived safely and were set for their first day at the Tyrrell. Then she'd try calling the mystery phone number she'd so cleverly procured. She excused herself and left for the telephone she'd spotted in the foyer.

After saying good-bye to her dad, Sam hastily pulled the scrap of paper out of her jeans pocket. As she began to dial, fingers gripped her shoulder making her spin around in surprise. Fumbling, she dropped the paper.

"Jackson!" Sam gulped. "You scared the bejesus out of me!" She reached down for the lost note, but Jackson was faster.

"Sorry, Sam." Then he glanced down at the number. "What's this?"

"Oh, nothing," Sam blurted. "Just the phone number of a friend." She snatched the note back and hastily stuffed it into her jeans.

"Well, you can try phoning your *friend*, but he won't answer," Jackson said with authority.

Sam was confused. "How do you know that?"

"Because *it's* closed until ten o'clock this morning." His cryptic answer added to her confusion.

"Do you know who this is?" Sam asked.

"I know *what* it is and so will you. It's where you're going to work." He continued his explanation. "*Museo* is Spanish for *museum*, and that number is for someone there."

"Spanish! You speak Spanish?" The articles on the museum thefts flashed through Sam's mind. What were the chances of bumping into two Spanish-speaking people here in Drumheller practically within hours of each other?

"*Si, muy bien, jovencita.* Where did you get the number anyway?" Jackson asked and Sam thought she heard a sharp edge to his question.

Not wanting to tell, she babbled on quickly. "Oh, I found it stuck in the pages of a book and wondered who it was. Is there something you wanted to ask me?" She batted her eyelashes innocently.

He hesitated, then changed mental gears. "There is. Since my car is in the shop due to a catastrophic mechanical failure, which is going to cost me *mucho dinero* to get fixed, I have the loan of one of the museum's field vehicles and I figured since we're going to be colleagues, I'd offer you two a ride. I know the first day on a new job can be a little intimidating and I'd be glad to supply encouragement and assistance." He bowed gallantly.

His offer was so warm and genuine, Sam felt herself relax. "That would be great. I'm not even sure where the Tyrrell is. It was getting dark when we arrived last night."

With perfect timing, Paige waltzed out of the dining room. "Jack, I couldn't help overhearing your offer. It's very nice of you. We certainly don't want to be late on our first day of a new job, do we Samantha?" she asked with all the brightness of a supernova.

"No, we sure don't," Sam said, matching the cheerful tone. "Thanks, Jackson. I'll get my backpack."

Sam thought about Jackson's ability to speak Spanish. One of the many useful things she'd learned from the Superior School for Spies was that there was no such thing as a coincidence, especially one related to a case. She patted the paper in her pocket. This could turn out to be a very interesting day.

Chapter 4

BIG JOB

The ride to the museum took them through a town that was obviously proud of its reputation as the dinosaur capital of Canada. As they drove, they were greeted by a colourful array of the extinct beasts placed alongside streets or posed proudly in front of businesses.

"Wow, Sam, that one's ginormous!" Paige gushed as a gigantic oversized replica of a *Tyrannosaurus rex* loomed into view.

"Hey, there's a viewing platform in its mouth!" Sam pointed up to the gaping jaws of the huge beast. "I bet visitors get a great view from between his teeth."

"The statues aren't what I'd call anatomically correct or to scale. What they are is fun and they really add to the feel of the town," Jackson informed them. "And since we're only now starting to get an idea of what colour dinosaurs were, the painting of each replica was left up to the owners. That's why you'll see a purple *Triceratops* or an orange *Stegosaurus*. Who's to say they weren't purple or orange?"

This started a lively discussion on what colours dinosaurs might have actually been. Sam argued that, since birds are descended from dinosaurs and birds are all colours, dinosaurs could have been as rainbow-hued as toucans or parrots.

"Your connecting birds to dinosaurs is right on target, Sam. In fact, it's now believed there were proto-feathers on most of the dinosaurs."

"Even *T. rex*?" Sam asked.

"Absolutely! He was king of the whole place and feared

nothing, so why not be as in-your-face as possible. Coloured feathers would also help him to attract a mate. Did you know they think some Tyrannosaurs hunted in packs? Can you imagine being chased by a herd of hungry beasts, each weighing more than eight thousand kilos and with teeth twenty-three centimetres long?"

Sam shuddered. Evolving millions of years after the dinosaurs became extinct had been a good thing for puny homosapiens. She found herself relaxing with Jackson and decided they'd simply gotten off to a rough start.

The Royal Tyrrell Museum of Palaeontology was located on the outskirts of Drumheller, and when they arrived, both Sam and Paige were blown away by the sprawling glass and concrete building.

"Wow," Sam whispered. "This is impressive!"

"And the design suits it with the earth tones and rockwork. It's so dino friendly," Paige added.

They drove around behind the large building to a door marked Employee Entrance.

Jackson held his security key card in front of the scanning device, and, as Sam and Paige watched intently, the door buzzed and obligingly unlocked. "You two will be assigned limited access key cards. Guard them with your lives. If you lose one, security will have your head on a pike. They're right over the top about these things."

As the three of them headed for the personnel office, they met an older gentleman in the hallway. "Good morning, Jackson. Who have we here?"

"Morning, Dr. Beech. These are two summer students, Samantha Stellar and Paige Carlson. Ladies, this is Doctor Beech, curator of the museum."

"Hello, Doctor Beech," they both said in singsong unison. Sam was reminded of little kids meeting their teacher on the first day of Grade One. She straightened, trying to look polished and desperately hoping she hadn't spilled anything on her shirt at breakfast.

Paige, ever the drama queen, struck a pose with one hand on the hip of her designer jeans, the red ones with the sparkly studded flowers on the back pockets, and offered her other to the curator. "Charmed, I'm sure."

Doctor Beech politely shook it. "Two budding palaeontologists, I dare say. Enjoy your stay with us, ladies, and if there's anything I can do to help, let me know." And with a chuckle, he continued on his way.

"Dr. Beech seems friendly," Sam commented as she followed Jackson down the hall.

"He's very easy to work for," Jackson said. "He lets everyone run their own projects without interfering or constantly monitoring them. It's a nice change from other places I've worked."

When they arrived at the Human Resources Office, the supervisor led them down a hallway to a room filled with filing cabinets and several desktop computers. "Paige, you'll be assigned to archive data. Your application said you were good with computers and had great keyboarding skills."

"Absolutely," Paige bubbled. "I haven't met a game console I couldn't conquer."

Sam had to agree. Paige's skills were legendary. She owed her talent to the million hours she'd spent playing video games on the free computers at the public library when she was supposed to be doing homework.

The woman was obviously pleased. "I'm sure you'll enjoy our new system. It's the latest and greatest. The program is set up; you simply fill in the blanks. You'll be transferring the information from those old card catalogues to the computer archives." She motioned to a row of file cabinets.

Paige took in the dozen battered steel cabinets. "All of those? There must be a zillion hours of data entry here!"

The woman was unfazed. "Don't worry. It's very user-friendly. You'll have no trouble."

Accepting her fate, Paige did what she always did – she made lemonade from lemons. "By the time I'm through here, my fingers will be moving at warp speed and I can really ramp up my score on *Neverwinter*. I couldn't have picked a better summer job." She gave Sam a crisp salute. "See you at lunch, Samantha."

Leaving Paige surrounded by the banks of cards and cheerily glowing computer screens, Jackson, the HR supervisor and Sam continued to the receiving area where Professor Caine, her new boss, waited.

"There's been a mistake," Professor Caine said gruffly as he pulled off his work gloves. He was tall, with a weathered face and grey beard. "I'm expecting a young man to help on this project. His name is, let me think. Oh, yes, Sam...Sam Stellar."

"That's me, sir. *Samantha* Stellar." She could tell he was less than thrilled with her explanation.

The professor curtly dismissed her. "You won't do at all. We've received a very important shipment from Colombia this morning and I need someone who can help with the uncrating and move the heavy pieces. This is hard physical work. I can't chance injuring a summer student who weighs only forty-five kilos."

Sam zeroed in on the part about her weight. She was no stick chick. Couldn't he see she was in fighting form? Then her brain registered the word *Colombia* and her heart skipped a beat.

This was the project she'd read about; the project she'd hoped for! She couldn't bail now. A super sleuth had to persevere. "Professor, if you'll give me a chance, you won't be disappointed. I'm quite capable of doing the work."

Obviously agitated, Professor Caine impatiently checked his watch. "All right, all right. I don't want any delays on this project. You can work with Jackson today. Keep in mind, if I hear any complaints, you'll be dismissed."

"Awesome!" Sam exclaimed enthusiastically. She was in! Then dialling it down to a more adult level, she added politely, "I mean, thank you for this opportunity, sir."

Professor Caine turned to Jackson. "Why don't you take *Miss* Stellar and get started. I'll be back in a few minutes." He and the woman from Human Resources left, and, as Sam watched, she could see Professor Caine speaking animatedly.

Probably setting up my replacement, Sam thought glumly as she followed Jackson to an adjoining work area filled with dozens of wooden crates. Her attention immediately focused as she saw Spanish writing on the boxes. If the crook wanted something South American from the museum, this shipment surely offered a nice selection.

"Don't let the professor get to you." Jackson interrupted Sam's mental case review. "He's the same with everyone, so don't feel he's picking on the new gopher."

Sam waited expectantly.

"You know," he explained, "*go-for-this* and *go-for-that.*"

"Great," Sam groaned. "A job that's really *going* places, if I get the chance and don't get canned on my first day."

"Professor Caine isn't the easiest person to work for. Still, I've always gotten along surprisingly well with him." Jackson offered her a pair of work gloves. "Like me, he hasn't been here long. In the past, he was tops in his field. In fact, he's still the go-to guy when it comes to these exotic fossils. And when the professor sent me to Colombia to work on this project in his place, everyone thought he was terrific. It was a real opportunity to study and will do wonders for my resumé. Between you and me, I think I was picked because I speak Spanish and could explain the shipping instructions, which were extremely complicated and involved huge amounts of paperwork."

"Your Spanish must be off the charts to have dealt with all those details."

"*Mi español es muy bueno.* I've worked on a few projects from that region and it really helps if you speak the language."

"I guess the museum is fortunate that Professor Caine accepted a position here," Sam said as she inspected a stack of smaller crates piled neatly by the door, noting the long number sequence on each box.

"You bet. Apparently, he and Dr. Beech are buddies from way back. The professor wasn't even on the radar, then out of the blue, Dr. Beech introduced him as the newest staff member. Quite a coup, actually, and he's probably the reason the Tyrrell got this fabulous dino." Jackson hefted a box and moved it to the work bench.

Sam paused a moment. "He must have professional credentials out the door."

"You bet. Professor Caine's past papers are university course standards. I haven't seen any recent publications, but he's legendary in the industry. Lately, he seems to have spent his time tracking down exotic finds such as our Colombian friend here." He patted the box.

Sam was shocked at this statement. "You mean there's an actual dinosaur inside all these crates?"

"I sure hope so," Jackson laughed, "or everyone's wasted a lot of time and effort."

Sam took in the room. "So this is how you ship dinosaurs from one place to another. It's a giant jigsaw puzzle with all the pieces individually wrapped."

"Right. And our job will be to put the puzzle together again."

"Why is the Colombian fossil so special?" Sam carefully ran her fingertips over a rough wooden crate.

"For two reasons," Jackson explained. "First, because the specimen is the only one of its kind found in South America and it's thought to be related to a species we have here called *Albertosaurus*. If it is in that family, it would be a major link between North and South America."

"And the second reason is…" Sam added helpfully.

"The second reason is the condition of the fossil," Jackson went on. "It's virtually a perfect skeleton. Every bone is accounted for. Extra care was necessary so none of the hundreds of bones went missing or were damaged in shipping. That is where my trip to Colombia came in."

Sam noted the rows of neatly stacked boxes. "How many people are going to be working on this project, Jackson?" She walked around one box that was nearly as big as she was.

"Eventually about a dozen scientists and technicians will be involved. For right now, Professor Caine says it's just you and me for the uncrating."

This surprised Sam. "You're kidding! Two people for all these crates?"

"One *people* and one *gopher*," Jackson corrected. "And Professor Caine, of course."

Sam puffed out her breath. "Then we'd better get started before the big guy gets back and fires the new gopher."

Chapter 5

X MARKS THE BONE

The small team spent the morning breaking open and discarding the crates as Professor Caine compared the contents against a complicated shipping manifest.

The dinosaur skeleton had come in burlap and plaster of Paris protective jackets with the bones encased inside. Some bones were still embedded in their original rock; others, mostly the larger ones, were already broken out.

Jackson and Sam had spent two hours loading a trolley with a crateful of smaller pieces when Professor Caine walked over to them.

"We're doing better than I expected," he said as he inspected one of the plaster-covered bones on the cart. "In fact, I'll get started on these and cross-check the bone count against the original data you brought back from Colombia, Jackson. You two continue with the uncrating." He pushed the trolley into an adjoining work area and started unloading the pieces onto a table.

Sam watched as Professor Caine carefully and almost lovingly laid out the small plastered items.

He was concentrating so hard, he never reacted when a page for him came over the public address system. Sam waited. After the third call, she had to do something and walked into to the work area. "Excuse me, Professor," she interrupted. "You're being paged to Doctor Beech's office."

"Not now!" he snapped, obviously annoyed at having his work interrupted. "What? Oh, the page. Was it for me?"

"Yes, sir," Sam added politely. "Dr. Beech wants you."

Muttering under his breath, the professor left to answer the summons.

Sam noticed Jackson was still hard at work on a large crate. Curious to see what all the small plaster jackets contained, Sam decided to be extra helpful and continue with the pieces Professor Caine had been working on. She hoped he would cut open the jackets after the sorting was finished, and, who knows, she might get a gold star for going above and beyond the call of duty.

The packing list was on the table with the fossils. Sam scanned the sheet, which told her these bones were vertebrae – part of the dinosaur's spine.

Sam read each fossil's long reference code. All the pieces had a complicated numbering system written on them. "I'm amazed at how carefully every piece is marked," she called to Jackson as she set a specimen in its correct numerical position.

"They have to be, Gopher." Jackson leaned on a crowbar trying to pop a board off his crate. "Or the bones could get mixed and the palaeontologists might reconstruct a dinosaur that belonged in a galaxy far, far away."

Sam scanned the room filled with crates and bones. "Wow, you could build an entire cast for a new sci-fi movie out of a dino this size."

"Right, which is why everything is so well documented from the initial find in the field right down to its positioning in a display." Jackson wrenched on the board and it groaned, then shrieked, as it splintered apart.

The noise was unnerving and Sam flinched. Taking extra, *extra* care, she went through the group of specimens she was working on.

The manifest listed one through twenty-three for the head to pelvis section; then the group of five pelvis bones and finally, the thirty-two vertebrae that made up the tail section of the spine.

The last and smallest pieces of the tail were the ones Professor Caine had been working on, and these Sam placed in their correct alignment on the wide table, then stepped back to survey the work. The spine would be perfect once the vertebrae were broken out of their protective plaster jackets.

Then she spotted it. There was another piece on the table.

Sam went over her sheets. All sixty vertebrae were accounted for. She recounted the column of bones. Nope, she hadn't made any mistakes.

Picking up the extra piece, she immediately saw there was something strange about it. Not only didn't it have the usual long reference number, the placement code was missing too. Instead, all it had was a black letter X written clearly on one side. She noticed another odd thing about the piece. Whoever put on the plaster jacket had done a really sloppy job.

Scanning the rest of the sheets, Sam tried to find a notation for the strange specimen. Everything had strings of numbers attached; none with the single letter X.

"Jackson, can you come here for a minute?" He walked over and she gave him the odd sample.

"What seems to be the problem?" Jackson inspected the piece.

"Don't you see? It doesn't fit, unless this dinosaur has a spare vertebra." She waited for him to continue his inspection. "Plus, no numbers. Only that X."

Jackson shook his head. "It doesn't appear to be a real fossil, Sam. Probably nothing more than an extra chunk of plaster." He gave it back. "Perhaps this is some Colombian palaeontologist's idea of a joke on us *Canadienses*. I'll take care of it later."

Sam watched him walk back to the crate he was working on. He was pretty certain about it not being a real fossil. Fine for him, except she was sure it really was something. Something important. She knew it. Her weirdometer was buzzing so hard it made her ears itch. She placed the extra piece next to the tidy line of vertebrae arranged on the table and went to join Jackson.

"I don't think the South American scientists would pull any crazy tricks with a shipment this important. And if it's only a chunk of plaster, why did someone take the time to mark it? I think it's an actual bone."

Jackson put his hammer down. "Okay, Gopher. You have one piece which doesn't fit or it could be a fragment broken off a larger piece. Don't worry about it. I said I'd deal with it." He went back to work.

Sam couldn't understand his casual attitude. For a scientist, he wasn't very curious. "I think it's important and I'm going to tell Professor Caine." She turned to leave, then Jackson's voice stopped her.

"All right, Sam, relax. Take it easy," he said. "I'll tell you what, it's lunchtime. Why don't you go, and I'll let Professor Caine know about this piece of plaster, which may or may not be an extra fossil."

"Promise?" She held up three fingers in a Scout salute.

"Don't worry. The professor will probably solve the mystery by breaking it open to see if it's real."

Sam decided there was nothing more she could do, and she was supposed to meet Paige for lunch. She went back to the work table and picked up the misshapen piece. As she turned it over, the plaster jacket moved. She shook the piece and it rattled faintly. There *was* something inside! A mystery fossil! When Professor Caine opened it up, she'd be proven right. Carefully, she replaced the plaster on the table. "See you after lunch, Jackson," she called as she left the room.

"Yeah, sure…lunch," he muttered, still concentrating on his task.

Sam was excited about her puzzling find. Wait till Paige heard about this! As she hurried out of the uncrating room, she ran smack into Doctor Beech.

"Oh, my gosh! I'm so sorry, sir," she apologized. Had Professor Caine talked Doctor Beech into canning her? Was he here to tell her she was going to be replaced on the project?

"No harm done," he said, straightening his suit coat. "Is Professor Caine back yet?"

Sam relaxed. He wasn't here to deliver bad news. "Not yet. Would you like me to find him for you?"

"No, no. Nothing that can't wait till after lunch," he said without urgency.

"That's where I'm headed now," Sam said.

"Then don't let me keep you, young lady. You'll need to keep up your strength if you want to be a good gopher."

Sam noted the use of her newly bestowed title. "I couldn't agree more, Doctor Beech." Her new employee jitters calmed, she felt like an accepted member of the team as she went to find Paige.

◎

The girls sat together at Paige's hastily cleared desk to eat their lunch. Paige listened attentively and was very interested as Sam explained all about the extra piece of bone, or maybe plaster, she had found.

"How do you know…" Paige took a large bite of the tuna and dill pickle sandwich Mrs. O'Reilly had made that morning, "…there's a bone inside?"

A sliver of pickle stuck to one of Paige's front teeth and Sam tried to avoid staring at the green glob. "I don't. What I do know is that it's shaped similar to all the other spinal pieces and it was included with them in the crate." She lowered her voice conspiratorially. "I think it's a mystery vertebra."

Paige continued chewing slowly and thoughtfully. Sam was reminded of a contented cow working on her cud. She loved her cousin. Who wouldn't?

Crunching noisily into a crisp, red apple, Sam wiped at the

juice dribbling down her chin with her sleeve. If their mothers could see them now, they'd be drilled in table manners for the next year. "I'm hoping Professor Caine will open the piece up and solve the mystery after lunch."

"That is, *if* there is a mystery, Sam." Paige gave her a look that spoke megabytes. "You said yourself; it could be a simple piece of junk plaster."

Sam waved her apple dismissively. "Yeah, yeah, I get it, no 007 stuff. But there's something inside. It rattled."

Her hand stopped waving and came to rest on the phone sitting beside their brown bag lunches. "Do you mind if I make a call?" she asked.

"Knock yourself out," Paige said casually as she checked her bag for more goodies.

Sam pulled the mystery phone number out of her jeans and dialed, then waited. This was her chance to crack the case wide open. (She was sure it was a case.) With a click, a canned voice came on the line announcing she had reached the office of Doctor Charles Feldman and to leave a message.

"Gottcha!" Sam crowed as she punched her fist into the air.

"What?" Paige asked. "Got who?"

Sam held up the slip of paper with the number. "The phone number I so cleverly procured belongs to one Doctor C. Feldman – the probable bone thief I'm tracking!"

Paige shook her head. "Sorry to break it to you, Girl Wonder, but I happen to know Doc Feldman can't be your dude."

Sam frowned. "Why not? This is the number Agent D wrote in the phone booth and it goes straight to Feldman's phone?"

"Because I had a question about an entry the doc made on one of my data cards and when I called him, I got no answer. I asked my supervisor if Doctor Feldman was on holidays and she told me he's been on a dig in Outer, or was it Inner, Mongolia for the past year and the switchboard must not have cleared his messages."

"Oh man, that sucks, big time!" Sam groaned. Dr. Feldman could not have been involved in any of this. Maybe she'd copied it down wrong, or the tracing wasn't clear. She shoved the slip of paper into her back pocket. Her best lead was gone... *big time!*

The rest of lunch was spent discussing what a dish Jackson Lunde was. Sam listened as Paige gave a detailed list of when he should ask her out, where he should take her, what she should wear and why the difference in their ages didn't matter...much.

Jackson was hard at work on a fresh crate when Sam returned.

"Hey Gopher, you're back early." He put his hammer down and yanked on a stubborn board.

"I thought I'd redo the vertebrae count before Professor Caine gets here. Not that I ever mess up, but hey, there's always a first time." Her casual laugh sounded a little nervous. She didn't want to admit to Jackson that she was the tiniest bit worried she was blowing this all out of proportion. After all, what did she really know? And relying on a strange feeling would hardly stand up in a court of law. "Did you talk to the professor about our extra bone?"

"Yes, I told him about the chunk of plaster before I went to lunch."

Something in Jackson's voice alerted Sam. "What's the matter?"

He hesitated only a moment, still it was enough to tell Sam he was not on her team. "Professor Caine was upset that you'd touched those fossils. He thought you might have mixed something up."

They both stopped talking as the professor hurried in. "Jackson, you said Samantha had discovered an extra vertebra for our dinosaur." He turned to Samantha. "Please show it to me now."

"Yes sir. It's right over here," Sam said with as much confidence as she could turn on. "It's beside the other fossils I've already put in numerical order."

She went to the work table where she'd left the bone.

It was gone.

Sam quickly scanned the carefully arranged pieces to make sure it hadn't been moved in among them. "I left it right here. Um...unbelievably, it seems to have disappeared." She turned to Jackson. "Did you see it?"

Jackson shook his head. "I got back from lunch a couple of minutes before you and started on this crate."

"Are you sure it belonged with the vertebrae group? Perhaps it's been put with another section." Professor Caine motioned to the entire room in case it may have teleported to some other part of the dino's skeleton.

"Although it was still encased in the plaster shipping jacket, it, it was the right size and shape to be a vertebra," Sam stammered.

Professor Caine inspected the neatly arranged display on the table, then went through the sheets Sam had used to set out the jumble of fossils and compared the numbers against the ones on the shipping jackets. When he'd finished, he shook his head. "Everything seems to be in order. Nothing amiss. You did a thorough job arranging these pieces. I'm actually impressed with your attention to detail, Samantha." His gruff tone relaxed. "If you're so sure the piece was an actual bone, I suggest you try to find it while Jackson and I continue unpacking the rest of the shipment. Perhaps it will show up."

Sam had the distinct feeling the professor didn't believe the piece was a bone at all. Jackson must have told him that it was merely a random piece of broken plaster.

She spent the rest of the afternoon scouring every inch of

both rooms. Frustratingly, by the end of the day the mysterious X piece still hadn't reappeared. She decided there was only one logical explanation.

While she and Jackson were at lunch, someone had stolen it.

It was exactly like the newspaper articles on the other museum thefts. They'd said odd pieces were removed, not entire shipments. With a shiver of excitement and her weirdometer registering nine on the Richter scale, Sam realized her case was developing rapidly.

The peculiar thing about this theft was that the piece stolen was still in its plaster of Paris wrapper. Whoever took it knew what it was and didn't need to wait for the jacket to be broken off. That must have been why it was marked with only the X.

Why that piece? One chunk of a dino, even an exotic imported dino, wasn't much good to anyone, unless... Sam remembered what Jackson had said about the uniqueness of this find. What if it was the proof that this type of dinosaur was the missing link with a North American species? If someone had the proof of that connection, it would be a very important chunk o' dino, indeed.

Professor Caine didn't seem the least bit worried that a potentially vital piece was missing. Sam decided his casual attitude must have to do with the way Jackson had treated the whole thing. Of course, the professor would listen to Jackson before her. She was, after all, only the gopher!

It was late in the afternoon when Professor Caine gathered up his paperwork and walked over to Jackson and Sam. "I'm going to finish this in my office. How's the rest of the uncrating progressing? Any more phantom pieces?" he asked Jackson with an obvious note of disbelief.

Jackson shook his head. "Professor, I know Sam believes the missing piece was a real fossil, but it was oddly shaped and not marked properly. It resembled a broken fragment of a shipping jacket more than anything else."

"Thanks for the vote of confidence, Jackson." Sam knew she sounded snotty and tried to dial it down. "Despite what you think, I'm sure it was the real deal."

"Samantha, I appreciate your concern that a specimen might be missing," Professor Caine said in a reassuring tone. "As a safeguard, Jackson and I have both gone over the manifest several times and also the import documents. According to those papers, all the pieces are here and accounted for."

Sam couldn't explain it. "If it was simply an extra piece of plaster, why did it have an X on it? Someone marked it for a reason." She could see neither of them believed that her find had been a real fossil.

Professor Caine noted the time on his watch. "It's late, and we're all tired. Let's call it a day."

Sam wanted to continue arguing her case, but knew when she was beat. Without another word, she reluctantly packed up her tools and then left.

◎

Paige was leaning against Jackson's pickup when Sam came out of the building. "How goes the bone business?"

"Terrible!" Sam shook her head. "Remember I told you about the piece with the X on it?"

"Yeah, the *spare spine*." Paige secured an errant lock of carrot-orange hair behind her ear.

Sam dropped her bombshell. "It disappeared over lunch."

Paige's head whipped around, sending the carefully tucked hair swirling like a fiery halo. "No way!"

"It's true. Jackson told the prof he saw *something*, then he said he thought it was probably a piece of broken plaster. Professor Caine thinks I have a faulty hard drive. As if! I know there was something inside that jacket. I heard it." She jerked the truck's tailgate down and sat on it. "I'm sure we won't find the piece because I know what happened to it." She took a breath and delivered her decision. "Someone stole it."

"Sam, you sound totally crazy. Why would anyone steal a chunk of junk?"

This was one reason Sam never worried about her cousin being sucked into some wacko cult. There was no way they could get her to switch to the dark side. *Sceptical* was Paige's middle name.

"It was *not* junk, cousin. Whatever was inside the jacket was important. Important enough for someone to sneak in at lunchtime, when no one was around, and steal it." Sam swung her legs back and forth agitatedly. "What other explanation is there? It was on the table before lunch; it had disappeared after lunch."

"Maybe it fell into the garbage." Paige hopped up beside her cousin. "And some hyper-efficient soul threw it out with the trash."

Sam shook her head adamantly. "No, I made sure everything was clean where I was working. There wasn't a garbage bin anywhere near the table." Suddenly, she grabbed Paige's arm. "O...M...G, to use an old expression!"

"What? What!" Paige squealed.

Sam pointed.

Walking quickly across the far side of the visitor's parking lot was a tall, dark-haired man she recognized. "It's *Agent D!*"

Chapter 6

MAN IN THE MIST

The next morning Sam was still mulling over Agent D leaving the museum scant minutes, okay, to be picky about it, several hours, after the mystery bone had gone missing.

The list of mega-coincidences in this case was long and, to Sam, there were simply too many to ignore: Agent D recently arriving in Drumheller and speaking Spanish – the national language of Colombia; Jackson going to Colombia to deal with this shipment and speaking Spanish (how convenient he was there to arrange the shipping of all these bones and could fluently explain to the Colombian bone dudes why he needed to add a piece to the shipment); this being the one shipment where a dino bone went missing. All of these pieces were connected, and Sam was going to find out how and why.

She was finishing breakfast when Jackson hurried into the dining room. "Ah, Gopher."

Sam placed her empty teacup carefully in the delicate china saucer. "That's me."

"I've got a seven o'clock appointment and won't be able to give you and Paige a ride to work this morning. Can you make it by yourselves?"

"Sure, Mrs. O'Reilly said she has two bicycles we can use, and the ride will do us good. Will you be coming in at all?" Sam was more than a little curious.

"Yes, but for how much longer, I don't know," he replied distractedly as he searched for the truck keys, patting his jacket, pants and shirt pockets.

Jackson's cryptic answer needed more explaining. "What's

that supposed to mean?"

Jackson withdrew his keys from his back pocket. "What? Oh, I mean, of course I'll be in later." He checked the time on his phone. "I've got to fly. Catch you later, Gopher."

Sam watched him hurry out the back door. Seven o'clock was a truly gross hour for a meeting. As she cleared away her dishes and prepared for the inevitable wait for her cousin, she wondered at the interesting bit of information Jackson had dropped. What was with the crack about not knowing how much longer he'd be coming to work?

The ride to the museum on Mrs. O'Reilly's ancient bicycles would be a challenge. The two-wheeled wonders were made out of steel and weighed a ton.

Paige saw their transportation and groaned. "You've got to be kidding! They don't even have gears!"

"Think of the great shape we'll be in by the end of summer." For a change, it was Sam's turn to keep a positive spin on things, even though it was going to be tough. She bent over and tightened the laces on her Vans. Getting her sneaker laces tangled in that nasty chain wouldn't do her, or the bike, any good.

"They must have cabs here. We can call a cab," Paige offered by way of a solution.

She was so hopeful, even Sam gave it some serious consideration. "One tiny problem. Neither of us has the money to pay for one without busting our budgets. So let's ride, girlfriend."

Backpacks strapped on, the two girls started the long commute to the museum. The day was bright and sunny, the air fresh, and by the time they arrived, laughing and wheezing, both decided it hadn't been that bad, in a health-nut sort of way.

◎

Sam was busily ripping crates apart when Jackson finally arrived at morning coffee break.

"Hey, about time you showed up," she teased. "How was your meeting with what's-his-name down at the..." She screwed her face up as though trying to remember something that was on the tip of her tongue.

"Oh, that. No problem," Jackson answered without giving up any information. "Anyway, it's a boss's prerogative to show up late and since I'm sort of your boss, I'm taking advantage of that workplace rule."

"*Hmmm*, my boss, huh? I'd say you are definitely bossy. Oh yeah, totally bossy," she teased back.

Jackson's tone became surprisingly stern. "This is the most important project I've ever worked on and Professor Caine is counting on me to make sure there are no screw-ups." Then, without another word, he picked up his hammer and started dismantling a nearby crate.

Sam was taken aback at Jackson's abrupt change, then she cut him some slack. He was right. This was a big deal, and she felt privileged to be in on it.

◎

Samantha decided to stay out of Jackson's way, which turned out to be a smart choice, as he was snarly to everyone. She wondered if it had anything to do with his early morning meeting. At lunch, she left for the computer department to find Paige.

"Are you nearly through? I thought we could snoop around the exhibits now and eat later." Sam hoped her cousin wouldn't waste this opportunity to tour the museum.

Paige added one last card to the stack she was working on.

"As a matter of fact, you're in luck. Done." She hit a key with an authoritative stroke.

Sam rubbed the top of the terminal thoughtfully. "Paige, can you tap into other areas besides the dino catalogues from here?"

"Yeah, I suppose, if I had the right password or access codes." Then she added suspiciously, "Why?"

Sam shrugged her slim shoulders. "Oh, no reason. I simply wondered what kind of wizardry you could perform on your magic box." She patted the CPU. "If you wanted to be a real pal, you could make a quick note of any codes that pop up."

Paige wasn't buying it, Sam could tell. "Not that I'm planning anything. Call it a quirk. When I'm on a case, I gather as much information as possible, whether or not it seems relevant at that particular moment."

Paige narrowed her fuchsia-mascaraed lashes. "Brilliant strategy, except for a minor detail. You're not *on* a case; you *are* a case!" Before Sam could continue, Paige scrunched up her face in a look of total pain...or disgust. "Okay, okay, enough with the drama queen stuff. You win. I'll gather never-to-be-used, unneeded codes, and I want it on my permanent record – *I'm the best cousin on the planet and a total superstar.* Now, let's go peruse those exhibits."

The two girls decided to make their way to the Cretaceous Garden Palaeoconservatory where present-day plants, similar to prehistoric ones, were grown in a giant glass atrium. To get there, they had to cut through the huge dinosaur exhibition hall. It was something to see, and they marvelled at the realistic dioramas and giant skeletons of fossilized dinosaurs. The reconstructed dinos were arranged as they would have been in life, standing over a kill, or guarding their eggs. Sam shuddered when she saw the size of the teeth and the killing claws capable of tearing through flesh with ease. There were lots of interactive exhibits to educate visitors in a fun way, and many were specifically geared to kids, making it very family friendly.

Finally, they arrived at the Cretaceous Garden and eagerly pushed through the glass doors. "I can't believe the size of these tree ferns!" Sam hooted as they entered the humid green space. "And the ivies and trailing moss are like a jungle."

Paige was busy reading a label beneath one of the plants. "*Sapotacea.* Hey, it says sixty-nine-million-year-old fossil pollen from this plant has been found everywhere in the world except Antarctica. Its modern counterpart gives us chicle, which is used in chewing gum. At last – evolution I can relate to!"

As they continued wandering through the large exhibit, Sam had the creepy sensation someone was walking over her grave. She was sure she was being watched. This was one spy skill she'd spent a lot of time honing. Gordon Craig, class nerd, used to sit staring at her in Language Arts and she always knew when he was doing it. Sometimes the feeling was so strong that the hairs in her nose would stand up, and she'd have to sneeze. Sam cautiously peered around. Nothing and no one.

A fine mist started to fall ensuring a high humidity level for the plants. Through the mini-monsoon, Sam caught a glimpse of a dark figure in a trench coat and black hat nearly hidden by the dense foliage. She blinked, refocussing, but he'd disappeared.

"Did you see him?" Sam whispered urgently.

"See who?" Paige grumbled as she held her purse over her head trying to deflect the tiny droplets. "If this downpour doesn't let up, my hair is going to self-destruct. Do they need to make it quite so realistic?" She stood under a screw pine tree until the mist let up. "Honestly, who expects it to rain *inside* a building?"

"There's someone watching us. I'm sure we're being followed." Sam quickly scanned for the exits, mentally planning escape routes.

"I told you, Sam – no more insane Spy School stuff! It gives me the heebie-jeebies." Paige shook the excess water off her faux-croc purse.

"I'm not kidding. Come on, we'll hide behind that fat sago palm and find out who it is when he passes us." She hurried Paige to the bushy plant that would offer them cover.

The minutes ticked by as the two girls waited impatiently. No one materialised. Carefully, Sam peered around the edge of the palm, hoping to catch a glimpse of her mystery man.

Finally, Paige could stand the waiting no longer. "Sam, there's no one following us. Your over-active imagination has OD'd again." She stalked toward the nearest exit, mumbling to herself as she went. "First secret messages in phone booths, then shadowy figures in the ferns. What next? Microphones in the lampshades?"

Sam was sure of what she'd seen. It had been someone tall, dark and, unless she was mistaken, South American. She ran to catch up with Paige. "I've got an idea who it was. Don't go all freaky on me, Paige. I think it was Agent D!"

Her cousin sighed in a way disturbingly like Sam's mother when she was completely out of patience. With the reminder of home Sam felt a fleeting stab of guilt. She'd promised her parents that she would play it safe and stay out of trouble if they let her go to Drumheller. Guilt was definitely not her thing, and besides, she wasn't in trouble – yet. Sam cut her cousin off before she could say anything. "I know you're revving up to lecture me on that 'no more secret agent stuff'. First, let me tell you something. The morning after we arrived, I was on my way to call the phone number I procured at the bus depot, when Jackson stopped me. He told me *museo* is Spanish for *museum* and the number was a local for one of the employees here."

"So that's what you meant by 'working on a case.' Rather a thin one, isn't it?" Paige flashed Sam her you've-got-to-be-out-of-your-mind look. "Some guy you see on a crowded bus, who may or may not have had a concealed hairbrush, writes down the phone number for a world-famous and wildly popular tourist attraction, and you turn it into a spy-vs.-spy thriller."

"He was a stranger here, and he wrote down the number for a *specific* individual at the museum, like you or me or *Jackson*."

"Right, Dick Tracey." Paige crossed her arms. "May I remind you *we* do not have a private phone number at the museum and it's not only Jack who does. Every permanent employee who's assigned to a specific section, people like Doctor Beech and Professor Caine and the janitor dude who cleans the washrooms, has a number. Besides, Jack didn't say it was *his* number did he?" She pushed through the exit doors of the Palaeoconservatory.

"*No-o-o-o...*" Sam drew out the word trying to think of a better comeback. The more she thought about the part Jackson had in this, the more her weirdometer went off. "Don't forget, he *was* the last guy to see the missing fossil piece before it vanished. He may have been cleverly throwing me off his trail so I wouldn't catch on to the big picture," she finished with satisfaction.

Paige whirled on her angrily. "There is no trail to be put off and no big picture. Jack's a nice guy, and I won't let you drag him into one of your phoney fantasies."

"Don't you see a connection? Jackson goes to Colombia and can speak Spanish. Our Agent D turns out to be Spanish-Speaking and I'm willing to bet a good old-fashioned loonie he's from Colombia!"

Paige shook her head. "That doesn't make Agent D a *spy* from Colombia; it makes him a *tourist* from another country. Big difference!" She marched off in the direction of the gift shop.

Sam watched as she strode away. The strong reaction to Sam's hinting Jackson was involved in the bone theft could mean only one thing. Sam had seen this before with her cousin.

Paige had a seriously stupid thing for Jackson Lunde.

"Great!" Sam knew this might complicate things if she

needed Paige's help in nailing her prime suspect and it turned out to be her cousin's latest crush.

She had a bigger problem. Even if Jackson was dirty, without proof she had nothing. She was a teenager with a history of being a little strange, and she was pointing a finger at a reputable scientist from a world-class museum. Oh, and the scientist was crazy cute, thought of her as the lab gopher and was not at all interested in Sam in "that way." No crown prosecutor in Canada would press charges. And on top of this, Sam would have to be extremely careful of what she said about the guy when Paige was around.

Chapter 7

ACID TEST

For the next couple of days, Sam watched and listened very carefully but the mysterious Agent D was either not around or was being extra careful not to slip up again. She didn't see any sign of him, in the ferns or out, and wasn't certain whether to feel relieved or disappointed.

Sam tried to keep everything in perspective. Okay, maybe she did have a tendency to jump off the deep end sometimes, and her cousin did dish out good advice, which meant Sam should listen to Paige's warning. But then she thought of all those coincidences piling up.

After a lot of sweat and aching muscles, Sam and Jackson had nearly finished the uncrating and cataloguing, and they were working together to organize the last of the bones into specific groups.

"So, Jackson, do you know where I'll be assigned next?" She pushed on an uncooperative block of securely jacketed bone. Even though she was in good shape, being rather small for her age meant that shoving plaster-covered chunks of dinosaur around was tough work. She gave the fossil one last shove and was rewarded as it slid into place.

"As a matter of fact, Gopher, Professor Caine and I already discussed your future. Since we're done with the uncrating, you'll be assigned to the Fine Preparation Lab to work on another project."

The idea of her being forced to leave what she was sure was the scene of the crime didn't sit well with Sam. Somehow she had to scare up more leads. So far, waiting and watching had done nothing to help her track down the bone thief.

Perhaps if she told Jackson about seeing Agent D in the conservatory, Jack's reaction might tell her whether or not there was a connection between the hidden lurker and himself. It was worth a try.

"Jackson, can I tell you something in strictest confidence?"

"Sure, Gopher, what's up?"

She leaned toward him. "I may be giving my imagination a free pass, but I think there's someone spying on us."

"Spying! What are you talking about?"

"Paige and I saw the guy here at the museum, at least I saw him," she corrected. "And I believe it's the same man who left the Spanish message in the phone booth."

"Phone booth?" Jackson asked. "You said you found the number in a book."

Sam cringed at having given that piece of information away. "I did – the phone book. Agent D, that's what we call him, sort of...left the ghost impression of the number, and I took a copy. Anyway, he was not only at the depot, he rode all the way from Calgary with us on the bus!"

Comprehension dawned on Jackson's face. "You were watching this Agent D, not me, right?"

"Right," Sam confessed. "The bigger question is, why was he there in the first place?"

Jackson betrayed nothing. "Maybe he's a visitor here to see the museum. It is a pretty popular place."

Sam shook her head. "He's no visitor."

"Did I hear you say someone was following you, Samantha?"

Professor Caine's voice startled Sam and she jumped. The old man had snuck up without her noticing. She had a lot of work to do on her sleuthing skills.

Not wanting to widen the circle of people who knew about her suspicions, or give her boss the impression she was paranoid, she cleared her throat and turned to the dour professor. "Actually, it's probably nothing more than my hyperactive imagination." She stuck her thumbs into her jean pockets, trying to act casual.

Professor Caine's gaze swept the room apprehensively. "All the same, someone watching one of my employees is not something we condone. I want you to tell me immediately if you see this person again and I'll have building security investigate at once. In the meantime, I'm going to keep you working here with me."

Sam wasn't sure if this was a good thing or a bad thing. She'd be staying close to the Colombian fossils, which was good, but she'd have Professor Caine watching her like a hawk, which was bad.

Later that afternoon Sam was helping Jackson put some of the catalogued bones into storage when she bumped a cart holding a large leg bone. The bone tumbled to the floor and rolled against a shelf.

Embarrassed at her clumsiness, Sam hurried over to the runaway fossil. "Hey!" she exclaimed, hefting the huge femur. "This thing hardly weighs anything. What gives?"

Jackson moved next to her. "It's a cast made out of fibreglass. Some original bones are too fragile, too unique or too heavy to use in the displays so fake ones are made." He tapped the replica. "They look exactly like the real thing and are easier to work with." He took the lightweight replica from Sam and replaced it on the trolley. "Never mind this stuff. I want to show you another of our palaeo-mysteries." He passed Sam a piece of rock with hundreds of tiny shells imbedded in it. "Every one of these shells is important and needs to be recovered. Guess how?"

Sam studied the fossil-studded rock for a moment then

gave it back. "Okay, I give up. How do you get the fossils out without smashing them to bits?"

"I'm glad you asked, Gopher. Right this way." Jackson swept his arm toward the door.

He led her down a series of hallways to an open room marked 'Noxious Laboratory.'

"Here in the *Obnoxious* Lab, we use special measures to free our little fossil friends." Sam followed him into the room and started to close the door behind her.

Jackson reached out and grabbed the door. "Whoa! *Read, then proceed* is my motto, especially here." He pointed to a sign Sam had missed on the way in. *LOCK BROKEN – DO NOT CLOSE DOOR!* "Maintenance is working on it – slowly. If I hadn't caught the door, we'd have been stuck. The lock won't open from the inside."

"Sorry." Sam felt foolish, then wondered what the big deal was. It was just a door. "I guess I was more interested in freeing 'our little fossil friends' than reading door signs."

Jackson ran his fingers through his hair in an irritated gesture. "Rule number one: In a laboratory, you have to pay attention. You could get hurt, and then my butt would be in the fire. I don't need any bad press because you messed up."

Sam thought he was way overreacting. She was sure someone would have come along and found them – eventually.

The Noxious Lab was dominated by a long table in the middle of the room on which lay a large partially exposed fossil. Sturdy workbenches ran around the outside of the room, with stainless steel sinks every three metres. Fume hoods hung down from the ceiling. On the walls were shelves with lots of different-sized bottles displayed. Sam saw they all had the corrosive warning label.

"Acid!" She loved the insider intel. "You use acids to dissolve the rock away from the fossils."

"So – you are observant when you want to be, Gopher." He

indicated the labels on the bottles. "I take it you saw those?"

"Yup, it's what clued me in, not to mention the peculiar smell in here." She wiggled her nose.

"This is one room that really needs fume hoods and you're right, we use different acids to leach out the fossils. The limestone cement in the rock dissolves, and then the palaeontologist can use his dental picks to finish cleaning the specimens."

"What types of acids are we talking about?" Sam asked, fingering the dark bottles.

"Careful, Gopher," Jackson cautioned. "Some of them are very dangerous. We use nitric and hydrochloric acids as well as glacial acetic acid."

Sam's brow arched. "*Acetic acid*, isn't that vinegar?"

"Right again!" he laughed. "It's not as dangerous. Unfortunately, because the acid is so weak, it's not as effective either. It still reacts with the lime in the rock so we sometimes use it."

Sam was starting to see that palaeontology was way more than digging old bones out of rock and she now understood the need for caution when working with fossils. Thinking about working with dangerous, or even lethal, acids made her nervous. Maybe Jackson hadn't overreacted after all.

Chapter 8

TIPS, TURTLES AND TREACHERY

Professor Caine had been more than watchful; he'd practically been Sam's shadow. It was nice of him to worry, even if it did put a crimp into her investigative work. And as for Jackson, she'd decided that even though he hadn't risen to her bait when she'd dropped the bomb about Agent D spying, it didn't mean he wasn't involved in something nefarious.

Sam thought *nefarious* was a great word. It sounded oddly Egyptian from the days of the pharaohs. *Bow, lowly slaves, when in the presence of Queen Nefarious.* Yeah, very cool, she decided as she and Paige bicycled home Friday afternoon.

"We have the whole weekend off, right?" Sam asked as they wended their way through the dusty streets back to the rooming house. The early July sun was so warm, she couldn't help wonder what the temperatures would be in August.

"Yeah, so?"

Paige threw her a suspicious look and Sam wondered what she'd done to warrant such mistrust. "So, after we check in with our parents, we have nothing too pressing, right?" She wheeled her bike onto Mrs. O'Reilly's street.

"No, Sam. I won't do it." Paige shook her head emphatically.

"You don't even know what I have in mind!" Sam protested.

"I don't need to hear any more. Whenever you open with 'Paige, we have the whole weekend off,' I know you've got a scheme bubbling up in that overworked brain of yours."

"Cousin! I'm deeply offended. My master plans should

never be referred to as *schemes*. They're well-thought-out, insightful *strategies* that can only be executed by a team of skilled operatives, such as ourselves." Sam leapt off her bicycle and pushed it up the gravel drive. "Besides," she added mischievously, "you haven't even heard this scheme yet."

Paige jammed on the brakes. "If it involves anything to do with your mysterious Agent D, count me out."

Sam opened the rickety wooden garage door and both girls walked their bikes in, being careful not to scratch Mrs. O'Reilly's car, although one more scratch would hardly have been noticed. The paint on the old relic was a little past its prime.

"All I'm asking is for you to come with me tomorrow on a short junket around Drumheller," Sam said in a tone that hinted at hurt feelings. "Not a big commitment for one cousin to make for another."

"Junket, shmunket!" Paige scoffed, then as though admitting the inevitable defeat, relented. "Okay, okay, stop with the Pound Puppy bit! As a matter of fact," she said thumbing through a non-existent appointment book, "until Mr. Right calls back, my social calendar isn't exactly full and, Lord knows, my thighs could use the extra exercise. Sitting all day slaving over a hot computer has got me thinking about secretarial spread." She twisted her head around at a bizarre angle and tried to watch herself as she walked away. "Tell me the truth Sam; do you think I'm getting hippo hips?" She continued her awkward method of locomotion until she tripped over the coiled garden hose.

"No Paige, for the ten-thousandth time! You're gorgeous, svelte, irresistible, mind-blowing model material. Now, about tomorrow..."

Sam was still explaining details for the morning's excursion as they sat in their room after calling home and before going downstairs for dinner. Paige listened absently as she inspected her Pucker-Pink fingernail polish for chips.

"I'm positive Agent D will lead us to the fossil. All we have to do is watch what he does, where he goes and who he contacts," Sam said nonchalantly. "No sweat!"

"There's one teeny tiny flaw in your master plan, Ms Bond. We don't know where this Agent D of yours is." Paige's voice held more than a dash of sarcasm.

"That's what my game plan for Saturday is all about. You see," Sam finished her explanation, "it's a game of cat and mouse, or mice and cat in our case." She sat back on her bed and folded her arms as though that explained everything.

"Let me get this straight," Paige said slowly. "You want us to cruise every hotel, motel and boarding house in Drumheller in search of the elusive Agent D?" She waited for Sam to confirm her suspicion.

Sam grinned at her cousin, showing all her teeth at once in a jack-o'-lantern creepy way.

Paige went on, the sarcasm still annoyingly evident. "Suppose he is a crook. He would, of course, have used his real name when he signed in and wouldn't mind at all if two busybody teens were to give him the third degree about his illegal business!"

"This is not my first rodeo, Ms Carlson. We're going to be a little more subtle than that. Leave it to me." Sam hoped her confidence wasn't *over*confidence. She had no choice now. She had to prove to Paige, and herself, that she wasn't dreaming this all up or blowing it way out of proportion. She wasn't a nut case...was she?

Saturday was a scorcher. By ten o'clock, half the kids on the block were already running through sprinklers. Sam and Paige started rather late on their quest for Agent D, mostly because Paige had refused to leave the security of her rumpled bed.

"Sam, we have to go back." Paige had pulled her bicycle over and was rummaging in her oversized purse/backpack/suitcase.

"Why? We haven't even investigated the first motel yet." Sam scanned the street up ahead for their intended target.

"Because," Paige said throwing her bag back into the bike basket, "I've forgotten my sunscreen, and you know, as a natural redhead, how paranoid I am about radiation sickness."

Sam took a deep breath. "Agreed, it's smart to worry about too much sun. In your case, I don't consider a barely-there tan radiation sickness. Squish your hat down over your ears and slip this poncho on. It will cover the rest of you till we get some lotion." She pulled a ratty green plastic rain slicker out of her own bike's ancient wicker basket. "Mrs. O'Reilly obviously believes in going prepared." Sam tossed the musty poncho to Paige who gritted her teeth before slipping it over her head.

They set out again with Sam in the lead and Paige reluctantly in tow. When Sam stole a glance at her cousin a few minutes later, Paige was pedalling at a furious rate. Her hat was pulled firmly down, and the mouldy rain slicker with its bright-orange reflective stripes merrily flapped in the breeze. Sam thought the total effect of the ensemble was hilarious.

"At least we won't have to worry about anyone identifying you, Ms Carlson. Your own mother wouldn't recognize you in your stylish new outfit."

Paige grumbled an inaudible reply and continued pedalling.

Drumheller was not exactly a huge urban metropolis and a complete tour of all the available lodgings consisted of a few motels, a hotel and a motor lodge, which was suspiciously like a motel with a restaurant stuck on the end.

"Let's do the east side first," Sam suggested, "then work our way through town."

"Why the east first? Have you used your sleuthing skills to

deduce something that will shorten this gross trip to the underbelly of crime?" Paige asked hopefully.

Sam shook her head. "Elementary, my dear Watson. It's all downhill from there."

The two girls wheeled into the parking lot of the first motel. Sam pulled a crumpled and stained letter out of her back pocket and a small notepad and pencil.

"Here, take the pad and pencil and follow my lead." She walked into the motel office and rang the bell at the desk. "Hello, is anyone here?" she called in a cheery voice.

A dishevelled woman wearing worn, pink clogs shuffled in from the back. Her faded, flowered dress hadn't seen the inside of a washing machine in some time. "Whaddaya want? You're interrupting my soap," the woman mumbled.

Sam watched in fascination as the cigarette between the woman's lips flapped up and down when she spoke. It was gravity-defying how the ember never flew off and set fire to the joint. "Uh, hello. My name is Marge Simpson, and I've been sent by my boss, Mr. Burns, to deliver this important message." She held out the crumpled letter.

The woman squinted at the envelope. "You can't read the name. The ink's all smudged. How do you know the person's here?" She lit a new cigarette from the butt of the first, blowing smoke out her nose in a great imitation of an angry dragon.

"I know the name is smudged, that's the problem. I got it wet by accident. You don't know my boss. He's a tyrant. If I don't deliver this, Mr. Burns will give me huge grief. I saw the gentleman in our office once, perhaps if I give you a description, you'll know if he's registered here." Sam waited as the scowling woman weighed her options.

"Okay, missy, hurry it up. I haven't got all day." The woman coughed, a thick mucousy sound, and spit into a used tissue, which she stuffed back into the pocket of the dress.

Sam went on hurriedly, "Thank you. The gentleman is quite

tall, has swarthy skin, dark hair and a thin, black moustache. "

The manager shook her head. "Nope, don't recollect anybody fittin' your description. Of course, Joe works nights. The gent might have come in then."

Sam noticed the staff used an old-fashioned book to check in guests, instead of a computer. "If I could peek at your register, one of the names might ring a bell. My boss said the fellow was Spanish, so perhaps one of the guests has a Spanish-sounding name."

"It's against company policy." The manager inhaled deeply on her cigarette.

Sam could hear background music on the TV building to a crescendo. "Gee, it sounds like something exciting is about to happen on your show." She reached out and tapped the register lightly.

The dishevelled woman slid a bloodshot eye toward the room with the music, then at Sam.

"Don't tell anyone I let you do this." She pushed the book across the desk and hurried back toward the beckoning sound.

"Score!" Sam flipped the pages. "*Hmm*, I'd say business hasn't been too good. This shouldn't take very long." She scanned the entries. "I'll call out any likely sounding names along with their room numbers and the license plates for their cars.

Paige waited expectantly, wiggling her notepad as if warming up the tires on a racecar.

"You know something, cuz? *Smith* seems to be a really common name around here." Sam continued running her finger down each page. "None of these sound right. I think Agent D is somewhere else." She reluctantly closed the book.

"Oh, well, we tried. Now can we go back to the boarding house?'" Paige squirmed as she adjusted her rain cape. She seriously resembled a Mutant Ninja Turtle.

"You're not thinking of bailing on me, are you? We still

have a whack of motels, the hotel and the motor lodge to scope out. Perseverance is the name of the game."

"I wish the game would be called on account of rain." Paige shook the voluminous cape. "I'm dying of heat in this thing."

"It will all be over soon," Sam assured her. "Then you'll be out of your misery."

"Do you have to put it that way?" Paige grimaced.

Sam called out a thank you as she and Paige left to continue the search.

"I must admit, your envelope trick was super clever, Sam," Paige complimented her cousin as they pedalled to their next destination. "You do seem to be cut out for this sneaky stuff."

"Basic operative procedure," Sam answered casually. She suddenly felt unreasonably happy at those few simple words and the vote of confidence they implied. Paige was her toughest critic when it came to Sam's dream.

The girls had the same bad luck with the next motels and then they found a Manuel Rameres staying at the hotel. Unfortunately, when *señor* Rameres showed up, he was not alone. There was also *señora* Rameres and four Rameres *niños*. He was definitely not their Agent D!

"There's only one more place he could be," Paige needlessly reminded Sam.

"It's a long shot and I don't care. We're going to do it anyway. We can't leave one stone unturned." Sam urged her bike toward their last destination, the Westgate Motor Lodge.

Chapter 9

PERSEVERANCE PAYS

Sam had finished her spiel about the waterlogged envelope and was going into a detailed description of Agent D when the desk clerk silenced her.

"Yes, it could be Mr. Delgato. However, I'm not allowed to tell you what room he's in without notifying him first. If you care to give me your name, I can call and let him know you're here," the clerk said officiously.

"Oh, don't disturb him," Sam said quickly. She really wanted to know what room Mr. Delgato, if that was his real name, was in. Pushing the crumpled letter toward the desk clerk, she added casually, "Would you please see that he gets this message?"

"Of course," the clerk said frostily.

"Thanks, 'bye." Sam turned, and she and Paige headed for the door. "Cut left behind this pillar and try to see what number the clerk writes on the note," she whispered out of the corner of her mouth. "I'll create a distraction."

The clerk wrote something on the note, then before she could put it under the counter, Sam windmilled her arms as she stumbled into a potted plant, knocking it over and scattering dirt everywhere. "Oh, my! How clumsy! I am so sorry!" she shouted loudly.

The clerk hurried from behind the counter and pushed Sam out of the way. "Don't walk through it! It will track all over the lobby. I'll clean it up. *Now leave!*"

Sam scurried for the door, reciting a litany of apologies as she went.

Ten seconds later, Paige emerged from the lobby.

"Two-zero-four!" she triumphantly informed Sam.

"You crushed it, cousin!" Sam slapped Paige on the back. "We know the room number if we need it. Now, since we have nothing better to do, let's just hang for a bit and see if Agent D goes in, or comes out." Paige groaned but decided to not object too much after her room-number triumph.

It was more than an hour later when a man left the Westgate and drove away in a blue, four-door sedan. "It's Agent D from the bus all right," Sam whispered as she peered through the hedge they were hiding behind. "The question now is, who's his contact at the museum." Sam read the license plate as the car left, committing it to memory. The numbers indicated it was rented. That would explain why Agent D had come to Drumheller on the bus and now drove a car. She also noted how he was dressed in dark clothes; he even wore black gloves and a black hat. Sam thought he could have been typecast as the bad guy in an old-time gangsta movie.

"This is what I call a good day's work." Sam elbowed Paige. "Not only do we know where Agent D is staying, we know the name he's using and the make and plate number of his car. This is even better than I'd hoped for." Satisfied, she started toward the back of the building where they'd stashed their bikes. "Wow, I'm starving. Let's return to H.Q. for supper."

Paige flapped her cape in an effort to cool herself. Her face was the same shade of fuchsia as her mascara and she was sweating profusely. Sam hoped she hadn't been too hard on her cousin by making her wear the cape instead of going back for the sunscreen. Who knew they'd be on her first stakeout so soon?

Supper was delicious and both girls ate way too much, then helped Mrs. O'Reilly with the dishes. Later, Rose Hocking dropped by their room and they talked late into the night. Rose told them stories about growing up in Wales and how she planned on staying in Canada permanently and hoped to become a Canadian citizen. Sam thought it was interesting to hear someone else's dreams for the future.

As they shared confidences, Sam was careful not to mention their day's activities, and for once, Paige clued in. Sam suspected it was because her cousin was too embarrassed to admit she'd spent the day in an old rain cape and hat, hiding in bushes and spying on every Tom, Dick and Garcia who'd remotely fit Agent D's description.

On Monday, work at the museum was progressing well, and Sam caught on quickly. If she were honest with herself, she had to admit she enjoyed the work. Palaeontology was a combination of educated guesses backed up with pure science, all wrapped up with infinite patience and a little luck. It was a lot like sleuthing.

Professor Caine continued to watch over her. Unfortunately, she had nothing concrete to report to him. She needed some hard evidence to connect Agent D and the missing fossil before she could go to the authorities.

Sam finished dealing with several crates of bones and headed to the project office with the paperwork. She put the sheets in the appropriate basket and was about to leave when she spied a corner of a file peeking out of a desk drawer.

Reading the title upside down wasn't hard. It was another useful skill that came naturally to her. Sam saw it was the original data Jackson had brought back from Colombia. Perhaps she could find some missed reference to the X fossil. She pulled on the drawer. It was locked. "Slithering snakes!" Sam muttered peevishly. "These people have a thing about locking doors, drawers and every possible carton or container in the building."

The desk was old, and the drawer didn't fit well. Sitting on the floor, Sam wedged a letter opener in the sliver-sized crack at the top, trying to pry it wider and wiggle the file out at the same time. As she fumbled with the file, the opener slipped and fell inside the drawer. "Oh, this is *so-o-o-o* not great!" It was then she saw a scrap of paper in the wastepaper basket beside the desk. Forgetting the opener, Sam retrieved the note.

The words scratched across it read *Delgato, Westgate Motor Lodge.*

This was the clue she'd been searching for! A positive connection. Someone at the museum was linked to Agent D, and she had a sneaking suspicion who it was.

"Is there something I can help you with, Gopher?" Jackson stood in the doorway.

Sam slammed the partially open drawer and hastily scrunched up the paper in her fist. She stood awkwardly, trying to cover her obvious actions. "Uh, no, I was dropping off these inventory sheets and tripped over my shoelace. I'm such a klutz. I guess I'll leave them...the papers...in the basket...on the desk. Right, that's done. I'd better get back to work." She edged toward the door.

Jackson continued to block the way. "Do you know what your problem is, Sam? It's the same one that killed the cat – it's curiosity. Except in your case it's plain old nosiness."

Sam gulped, then tried to push past him.

"I wouldn't go poking around for trouble, Gopher. You might find it."

"Me? Trouble? No way," Sam replied a little too quickly.

He gripped her shoulder. "The missing piece of plaster you're so worried about – that's all it was – *a piece of plaster.* Got it?"

Sam shook him off, then tried to be cool. "Yeah, I know you're right. Sometimes I let my imagination run away with me. My focus now is this great summer job. It's all I care about. Well, duty calls." She squeezed past him and hurried down the hall.

Jackson was being a first-class jerk. He was also really scary. It was far too late for her to pull out of this case. With a little luck, Jackson Lunde would think his warning had worked, and she'd backed off the missing fossil thing. When she was around him, she'd be sweet as Saskatoon pie and as innocent as a babe. Unless she had to weasel something vital to the case, and then she'd be very, *very* careful how she did it. In the meantime, she was going underground.

For the rest of the day Sam studiously avoided Jackson. His spooky behaviour in the office was hard to shake but by quitting time, she was sure he had swallowed her act. Heck, she'd been so helpful and sugary, even she believed the show.

A half-hour before quitting time, Jackson took off his lab coat and hastily gathered his paperwork. "See you tomorrow, Professor. 'Bye Gopher."

He left, and Sam wondered where he was off to in such a hurry.

"Samantha," Professor Caine called, "these fossils must be safely put away before we go home." He indicated a cart laden with the fossils he'd been working on. "Would you mind returning them to the storage area while I take the catalogue sheets to the computer room?"

"No problem, Professor." Trying to make it seem easy, even though the wretched thing weighed a ton, she pushed the heavy cart into the huge storage area.

It was dark and Sam had trouble finding the section she wanted among all the shelves and stacked crates. At last she found the assigned shelf. "Wouldn't you know it, right on the top!" She moved a stepladder over and started ferrying the heavy boxes up to their lofty perch.

Struggling, Sam had just finished tucking the last box into

its slot when she heard a noise behind the tall stack of crates across the aisle. She froze.

"Who's there?" The silence was ominous. Quietly, she climbed down from the ladder.

Suddenly, there was the sound of scraping boards and Sam's head snapped up in time to see a tower of heavy wooden crates teeter and sway in her direction! She gasped and threw herself out of the way as the whole pile came crashing down.

Wood splintered, choking dust enveloped her and the noise was deafening! Rolling out of the way, Sam thought she saw the storage room door close behind the dark outline of a man.

All the clamour brought technicians scurrying from the adjacent labs.

Professor Caine pushed through the crowd. "Oh, my God! Samantha, are you hurt?" He helped her stand, concern etched on his weathered face.

'No. At least, I don't think so," she stammered. He reminded Sam of a worried Santa Claus.

"You must have bumped the crates with your ladder, Gopher."

Jackson's voice made her whirl around.

He inspected the pile of heavy boxes. "You had a very close call."

"I never touched those crates!" Sam's voice cracked rather foolishly as she spoke.

"Jackson, find a seat for Samantha and get her some water. I'll take care of this…" Professor Caine waved at the shattered boxes, "…this destruction."

Jackson led Sam back to the uncrating room as the professor directed the clean-up.

"I thought you'd gone for the day." Sam couldn't catch her breath or calm her racing heart. Jackson brought her a chair and she was grateful to sit; her legs were doing the no-bones thing and didn't want to hold her up any more.

He offered her a bottle of water. "I was on my way, then I heard all the fuss and came to see what happened. That was a nasty accident."

Sam didn't say anything as she took the bottle. She wasn't sure if *accident* was the right word to use.

Chapter 10

POINTING FINGERS

Mrs. O'Reilly walked into the dining room carrying a thickly frosted birthday cake aglow with candles. The cake was for Rose, who beamed as everyone at the table sang an enthusiastic, if off-key, chorus of "Happy Birthday." Sam and Paige had decided Rose was cool. It was easy to laugh with her.

"Thank you all so much!" Rose said after the singing had subsided and she'd extinguished the candles. "This truly means a lot to me. You are all the family I have here in Canada, and I don't know what I'd do without you." She stole a shy peek at John.

"Would it be impolite to inquire how old you are today?" Danny asked, as Rose cut into the confection.

"Not at all." Rose added a little extra frosting to Danny's piece before giving it to him. "For everyone's information, I'm twenty-five today. I came to Canada right after I graduated and was lucky enough to be hired by the brokerage firm I work for now. I'm 1.63 metres tall, weigh eight stone, that's about fifty-one kilos for you colonials, and have all my own teeth. Any other questions?"

Everyone laughed, and happy, noisy conversation soon followed as the heaping plates were passed around. The LaSalle sisters always dressed for the evening meal, but Sam thought the two fragile ladies had outdone themselves tonight. "I must say, Abigail and Clarisse, you two are both stunning this evening," she said.

"Thank you, my dear. How kind of you to say so." Abigail's voice was soft as face powder. "Clarisse and I think birthdays are special, especially birthdays that aren't ours. We've had enough of them, thank you."

Sam, who was in charge of filling everyone's cup, poured more tea. When she offered to top up Paige's, her cousin covered her cup with her palm.

"Whoa! No thanks, Sam. I'm tea'd out. Think I'll get a pop."

She left for the kitchen and Sam was about to offer Jackson and John refills, when she heard something that made her hang back.

"Jackson," John said setting his cup down. "You missed being there for your big transfer today."

Jackson didn't say anything.

John went on. "As a matter of fact, it's the biggest deposit I've ever put through."

"Today's deposit?" Jackson asked quickly. He stirred his tea so hard it sloshed into the saucer.

Sam listened with interest as she offered Clarisse milk or lemon.

John lowered his voice and leaned toward Jackson. "Yes. It's not every day I get a ten-thousand-dollar transaction, especially when it's a transfer to a friend."

Sam nearly dropped the sugar cube she was offering Abigail. *Ten thousand dollars!* Who forgets a ten-thousand-dollar deposit to their account? She slid a quick peek at Jackson. He was speaking so rapidly and quietly to John that Sam couldn't make out what he was saying.

Later, after helping Mrs. O'Reilly tidy up the mini-birthday party, Sam, Paige and Rose took a leisurely stroll, enjoying the warm evening air. Walking around the sleepy neighbourhood, Sam mulled over the newest clue of the complicated case. The money deposited into Jackson's account today had been a sizeable chunk of change.

"You're such an open book," Paige teased, watching her. "I know what you're thinking."

"I didn't know mind reading was one of your many talents, cousin." Sam stopped to breathe in the heady fragrance of the lush trees. It smelled green; at least that's how she'd describe it if a colour had a scent.

"How long have I known you Samantha Stellar?" Paige, waited for Sam to finish sniffing the foliage. "Don't you think I know that if there's even a whiff of mystery in the air, you're going to be freakily focused on it? You're thinking about all the so-called clues you've been collecting and the missing bone with its connection to Agent D, who we saw leaving the parking lot scant minutes after its disappearance."

"It was a little more than scant minutes, Paige Carlson," Sam corrected, knowing Paige had nailed it.

Sam had tried to stop her mind from going over everything, which was impossible as her detective's brain kept replaying the details of her dinosaur dilemma. There were so many odd things tied in with the case.

"What are you two going on about?" Rose asked turning back to join them.

Paige, whose Facebook page was like gossip-girl central, eagerly explained, "Rose, you won't believe what's been happening. Sam, apprentice super sleuth, has uncovered a ready-made mystery at the museum."

"Wait a minute. A real mystery or a wished-up mystery?" Rose sounded extremely sceptical.

Sam wasn't sure if telling Rose was a good idea. There wasn't any real proof of anything except a note about where a foreign visitor was staying, and she didn't want to be labelled a nut job to a whole new group of people. "Paige, maybe we shouldn't say anything yet."

"Half a minute," Rose said. "If you really are onto something, maybe I can help. Our brokerage firm does the importing for the museum and I process all the documents for the shipments."

Sam was surprised at this answer. She expected Rose to

give her the run-along-and-play-crazy-girl speech, like everyone else did when it came to the secret plot and dastardly plan
stuff. This said a lot about Rose, and Sam found herself thinking
perhaps another brain working on the problem would help.

A leap of faith was called for, so Sam took a deep breath
and jumped. "Okay, I'll tell you everything I've been able to
piece together. First, I believe a felon from Colombia is here in
Drumheller. I think he came in on the bus with Paige and me."

"We tracked him down during what I refer to as the *Saturday from Green Vinyl Hell*," Paige added.

"You're going to get a lot of mileage out of that poncho,
aren't you?" Sam shot a silencing glare at her cousin. "As I was
saying, this Agent D, as I tagged him, is up to no good. He had
a museum employee's phone number and I'm sure he was spying on Paige and me when we went through the Palaeoconservatory." She took a breath. "You see, Jackson and I have been
working on this super-important, rare fossil find from Colombia."

"Yes," Rose said. "I remember doing the import documents
for the shipment."

Sam went on, "I went over the vertebrae bones and came
up with one extra piece."

"Which might not have been a real bone," Paige put in.

Sam ignored the interruption. "Rose, you know how carefully this stuff is recorded. An extra piece simply wouldn't be
there by accident."

"True," Rose said. "Still, there were a lot of pieces and
sometimes things break apart during transport. We are talking
fragile fossils seventy-five million years old. So, if an item were
to be put in after the shipment was prepared, no one would
have known, especially if it appeared the same as all the others."

Warming to the direction their conversation was taking, Sam
continued, "A fragment that had broken off another chunk is

totally possible, except my piece hadn't broken off. I'm sure of it. It was clearly marked with an X. The extra bone was left on the table, and Jackson said he'd tell Professor Caine about it. I left for lunch and when I came back, it was gonzo. Disappeared into the ether! *Poof!*" She waved her arms like a magician.

Rose ignored the theatrics. "Go on."

"Later, as Paige and I were waiting in the parking lot, we saw Agent D's car leaving in a screaming big hurry."

"Tell her about your near brush with death," Paige prodded helpfully, and Sam half-regretted telling her cousin about the earlier mishap with the crates.

"I wouldn't call it that exactly. It was a little scary though." Sam tried to make her voice sound nonchalant.

"What happened?" Rose asked, alarmed.

"It went down like this…" She kept her voice very matter-of-fact as she ran through the details. "I was putting a box of fossils away on a shelf in the storage area, when this huge stack of heavy wooden crates fell over. I had to dive out of the way, or I would have been crushed."

"Squashed as in bug-on-the-windshield-of-a-Hummer," Paige added.

"Jackson was supposed to be gone for the day, then he materialized out of nowhere…" She let this hang in the air a second too long before going on. "I thought the timing of the accident at the museum was suspiciously close to when Paige and I tracked down Agent D. He's staying at the Westgate Motor Lodge, room 204, in case you need to know for the police statement," Sam clarified.

Rose raised her perfectly plucked brows. "Oh, Sam! This is the first I've heard of this. How odd Jackson never said a word when I was speaking with him. I'm so glad you were unhurt."

Paige poked her finger toward Sam. "Sam is certain the chances of that particular stack of crates picking that particular moment to fall are about as improbable as her winning

Miss Congeniality."

"So, what are you saying, Sam?" Rose's voice now had a note of apprehension.

Sam had to tell her. "I'm saying this Colombian Agent D bone-thief has inside help from someone at the museum. I think that someone is Jackson Lunde." Sam avoided Paige when she said this. "He's the only common element. He was in Colombia earlier this year working on this project; he was on the same bus as Agent D and he was alone with the X-bone before it zapped off. Plus, he's been acting strange." She thought of the warnings and veiled threats Jackson kept giving her.

Rose was silent as Sam continued.

"After I spotted Agent D at the museum, Paige and I spent the next Saturday tracking him down to discover where his base was. Right after we did, someone arranged the accident with the crates. I believe it was Agent D. He must have figured out I've been investigating him. I've also been expanding my search for clues to the missing fossil," she added casually.

"How?" Paige asked quickly, recognizing Sam's oh-so-casual comment as the tip of a sneaky iceberg. "You didn't tell me about this."

"You should think about getting into the spy business yourself. You never miss a thing." When it came to secrets, Sam knew her cousin was like a bulldog with a bone. No way could Sam duck out now. "The plot is thickening. I was in the project office trying to jimmy a locked drawer to get at some confidential paperwork, when I found a note with Agent D's name and motel on it."

Paige's mouth worked, but no sound came out.

"You were trying to break into someone's desk?" Rose asked incredulously.

"More like seeing if it was securely locked. It doesn't matter 'cause I never got into it. Jackson interrupted me before I could make much progress."

"You were caught!" Paige croaked.

"Well…not exactly. I hadn't quite busted the drawer open when Jackson showed up."

Rose pursed her lips as she tried to unravel all she'd heard. "Wait, back up. How did the fossil get lost in the first place?"

"It wasn't lost, it was stolen from the table in the workroom and it all happened so quickly, no one had time to cut open the jacket to confirm that it was an actual fossil and not a piece of plaster. This is very convenient for Jackson because now he can say he saw it, and it was only junk anyway," Sam went on in a rush. "Everyone sort of forgot about it, treating the whole thing as the ravings of a fanatical teenager with a hyperactive imagination! I think Agent D ordered Jackson to steal the fossil before anyone else saw it."

Paige and Rose both listened, speechless as Sam finished her story.

"And I believe," Sam continued, "the piece has been, or will be, smuggled to Agent D who's been waiting for it since he came to Drumheller. It wasn't listed on any of the documents I saw. Maybe when Jackson was in Colombia, he marked it with the X so it would be easy to spot – and easy to grab."

"As a matter of fact," Rose said thoughtfully, "there was a small hiccup with the paperwork on that shipment, and I had to go over every blasted number. I don't remember any fossil designated with an X. Believe me, my brain hurt from the long number sequences and a solitary letter or number would have jumped out at me."

Sam's head hurt from all the thinking. "So there's no proof it was anything more than a chunk of broken plaster, which is how, at Jackson's suggestion, everyone's treating it. I'm sure there was something inside. The problem is without the piece, I can't prove anything."

Paige squinted angrily at Sam. "This is the dumbest thing you've come up with yet. You're accusing Jack with only a boatload of circumstantial evidence. He's not some low-life, petty thief! He's a kind, generous and honest guy." She crossed her arms. "And why would he want to steal it in the first place? If he can prove that bone is the missing link thingy, he'd be famous."

"He needed it so he could sell it to Agent D for ten thousand dollars." Sam's voice was little more than a whisper, but from the way Paige and Rose reacted, she may as well have shouted.

"What ten thousand dollars?" Paige sputtered, having a little trouble keeping up with Sam.

"The ten thousand deposited into Jackson's account today." Sam nearly winced when she said this.

"Why didn't you tell me?" her cousin demanded.

"Because I only found out about it tonight," Sam shot back.

"How do you know about the money?" Rose asked.

"I overheard John congratulate Jackson at the table about his ten-thousand-dollar deposit today. It was John's biggest transaction ever." Sam could feel sweat on her forehead. This was weird because she hadn't done anything, really. Was this gruelling grilling even legal under the Canadian Charter of Rights and Freedoms?

"And where was I when this was going down?" Paige interjected.

"You'd gone to get a drink. You said you were tea'd out. Maybe it was teed off." Sam was at the end of her patience.

"You think Jackson set this whole thing up when he was in Colombia arranging the shipment." Rose's comment was more of a statement than a question.

"It all fits, and the evidence does point that way." Sam could practically feel Paige's temper ramping up.

"I still don't believe it!" Rose shook her head emphatically. "I know Jackson. Surely, he wouldn't do such a thing."

"It's only a theory." Sam turned to Paige, hoping to dial

down her cousin's anger. "I'm not going to say anything to him. And I don't think anyone else should either, not until I've had a chance to gather more evidence."

"I wouldn't think of repeating such a barrel of cow manure!" Paige growled through clenched teeth before stomping away.

Sam sincerely hoped her cousin would stay quiet and not blab any of this to Jackson. She and Rose continued walking in silence.

After a while, the soothing magic that accompanied the peaceful evening did its work and Sam changed the subject. "Rose, do you mind if I ask you a personal question?"

"Depends. Try me and we'll see."

"I couldn't help noting you're fond of John. So why don't you two ever date?"

"My, you are observant, aren't you?" Rose said, surprised. "The answer is quite simple really. He hasn't asked me."

"Okay, he hasn't asked you..." Sam waited a beat. "So why don't you ask him? This is the twenty-first century; a girl doesn't have to wait for a guy to ask her out. If she wants to hook up with him, she should go for it. There are lots of sassy girls who've made the first move." This was true, even if Sam wasn't one of them. Regrettably, no guys had made a move on her either.

"Where I was brought up, a lady doesn't ask a fella out. I don't want to seem too pushy, or worse, too desperate," Rose said in her own defence.

"This isn't Wales, Rose, and you know what they say. 'When in the colonies, do as the colonials do.'" It was pretty simple to Sam.

"I'll think about it," Rose promised. "Except..."

"Except what?" Sam picked a leaf from a bush they were passing and smelled the freshness.

"Except – what if he turns me down?"

The lack of confidence in Rose's voice was obvious, and Sam felt she had to help. "Then you'll have to try harder – razzle-dazzle him, or at least wear him down. No one in their right mind would ditch you."

They'd caught up to Paige, and Sam offered her the leaf in lieu of an olive branch. "Besties again?" she asked hopefully.

Paige took the green tidbit, stuck it in her mouth and chewed viciously before swallowing.

At the boarding house, all the lights were off. The trio said good night quietly and crept off to their beds.

Sam lay sleepless for a long time watching the shadows dance on the ceiling. "Paige, are you still awake?" she whispered.

"No." The terse answer came from under the covers on Paige's bed.

"I know you're ticked off with me about Jackson..." Sam wasn't sure her cousin understood the big picture. "You're simply not looking at the facts logically."

Paige poked her head out from under the duvet. "*I'm* not being logical! *You're* not being realistic. Jack is star material and wouldn't think of doing anything crooked." She waved perfectly manicured fingers in Sam's direction, silencing her. "I know, your so-called evidence – Jack going to Colombia, Agent D *probably* being from Colombia, Jack being the last person left alone with the fossil before it disappeared, and, of course, the ten thousand dollars. All circumstantial, which is what any good defence lawyer would say." Her voice was rising at an alarming rate. "You, girl, have no faith in your fellow man...or guy." She punched her pillow and then flopped back down on it.

Sam remained quiet.

"Well?" Paige's tone left no doubt as to how angry she still was.

"I'm thinking," Sam said. "And you know what I'm thinking?"

"I couldn't begin to guess with the way that twisted little brain of yours works."

Sam ignored Paige's dig and propped her head up as she leaned on one elbow. "Jackson's a cool guy. I don't want him to be a crook either."

"*A-r-r-g-g-g-h!* Paige groaned. "What about the stupid *evidence*?" Paige's voice was a little strangled, which was probably what she wanted to do to Sam.

"I know, I built the case, remember? I have a weird feeling, as though we're missing something, something right out in the open I can't quite put my sticky little fingers on. I need more intel to put this whole thing together."

"Great! First you throw him under the bus with this airtight case, practically convicting poor Jack, and then you flip-flop on it because of a weird feeling? Come on, Sheriff, make up your mind." Paige halted mid-tirade. "If all this is real, then there's something you should worry about, Sam. Whoever stole the bone probably arranged your accident and could arrange another you might not walk away from."

Ignoring the obvious danger, Sam sat up. "There's only one thing left to do."

"What now, the RCMP? The FBI? Spiderman?" Paige pulled her newly fluffed pillow over her head.

"No, Furbrain. I have to find that fossil. Find the bone and we find the answers. Answers that could explain Jackson's involvement, maybe even clear him." Sam rearranged her own pillow in an effort to lessen the lumps.

"We know Agent D already has the fossil. We saw him leave with it."

Paige's logic was less than flawless.

"Nope, cousin, we saw Agent D *leaving*. We don't know he had the fossil. It could still be at the museum. In fact, if I were trying to hide a fossil, I think a museum full of fossils would be a pretty darn good place to stash one." Sam thought about this, liking it. "If Jackson did take the fossil…for whatever good reason," she added quickly trying to keep Paige from going ballistic again, "he almost had to hide it at the museum. He didn't go home over lunch. Then there was the gong show I caused, and with everyone watching everyone, Jack wouldn't chance having it found on him. He'd hide it somewhere in the building until the heat died down, and it was safe to remove the thing."

"And if he *didn't* steal it, which one of us is sure he didn't, you're off on another wild goose chase." Paige's disembodied voice came out of the darkness.

The more she thought of it, the more positive Sam became that the key to solving this case was to find the missing bone. No sense in waiting. She'd start her search right after work tomorrow.

Snuggling farther down under her comforter, Sam tried to shut off her brain and sleep. She'd need her rest if she wanted her investigative powers to be working at one hundred per cent tomorrow night.

Chapter 11

NEEDED: ONE GRUMPY ALLY

"Come on Paige, we're late!" Sam picked up her lunch bag, then felt in her pocket to make sure her security card was there. Without the magic card, she'd be unable to get into the building or half the rooms in it.

"Okay, let's go, go, go!" Paige rushed past, frantically clutching at her sweater as her purse slid off her shoulder and her lunch bag ripped. Cursing, she stuffed the torn bag into her purse as they raced out the door.

The trip to the museum had both girls pedalling the old bikes as hard as they could. The early morning air was crisp and clean, making Sam feel great. She gawked around at the fanciful dinosaurs, the quaint shop fronts and the general small town appeal of the place. Drumheller was a picturesque prairie town, and Sam appreciated the chance to spend her summer here.

She refocused on the road, narrowly missing a nasty pothole that leapt out in front of her. Clanking along behind, Paige swerved to the other side of the crater and also avoided a disaster.

"Yee-haa!" her cousin crowed as though making it to work without a mishap was a personal challenge to be won.

"Woo-hoo!" Sam yelled in response. The sky was electric-blue, the warm wind blew through her long hair...she felt awesome! Life was a wonderful journey, even if there were a few potholes in the road.

When they finally screamed into the parking lot at the museum, they were flushed and out of breath.

Jackson had gone on another of his mysterious morning meetings, which meant Sam was already hard at work when he arrived.

"Morning, Gopher," Jackson greeted her as he slipped on his lab coat. "Hey, I was wondering, anything new on the phantom fossil front?"

Playing dumb seemed the best and safest course of action to Sam. "Nope, *nada*. I guess it's gone for good. It doesn't matter anyway. I'm sure you were right. It was probably nothing more than a piece of plaster that broke off some big old bone." She deliberately kept her tone light.

"Now you've got it, Sam. I'm sure it was garbage that should have been thrown out in the first place instead of causing all that excitement." Jackson added some papers to a file folder on the desk. "It's a good thing nothing showed up missing on our manifest. Disappearing fossils are treated seriously, and I'd hate to have an investigation going on while we're trying to work."

Or perhaps, he'd hate an investigation at any time, Sam thought. "What would happen if it turned out some person, say someone who worked here, deliberately stole the fossil?" She could have bitten her tongue. From the way this got his attention, she knew she'd thrown a red flag.

"I don't know who would want to steal one bone but if he, or she, were caught, the matter would immediately be turned over to the police. Good thing it was only a piece of plaster."

Sam thought she saw a suspicious glint in his baby blues as he walked away, then chalked it up to a trick of the light or, she admitted a little guiltily, a trick of her imagination.

Give the devil his due; Jackson was sure chill. Because she was a grade A blabbermouth, Sam had practically told him he was her main suspect and he hadn't even flinched.

Her co-worker loaded more bones onto a cart near his sorting table. "I'll put these in their proper bins in the storage area.

That way nothing more, real or imagined, will go missing."

Had she heard a condescending note in his voice? Whatever it was, it pressed Sam's irked-off button. She'd love to take this conversation to the next level, which, she was sure, would only lead to trouble. She recited her new mantra: "Keep a low profile, keep a low profile." Goading Jackson into answering wouldn't do any good. If he was guilty, he sure wouldn't say anything helpful. If he wasn't, then she'd come across like she was on a witch hunt with poor Jackson the main candidate for burning.

Backing off was the best and smartest course of action. Retreating to a far bench, she studiously continued sorting specimens and was quietly working when Professor Caine came in.

"Samantha, any problems?" he asked kindly.

"No sir, everything is under control." She hesitated, holding a half-filled box of bones. Pretending to back off from Jackson was one thing, but she was still hot on the case and needed answers or perhaps an ally. "Professor Caine?"

"Yes?" He continued reading the file he'd brought with him.

"I've been giving the missing fossil some thought and I don't think we're going to find it." Sam's palms felt sweaty and she gripped the box a little tighter.

"You never know, Samantha. Things have a way of turning up, even odd pieces with an X on them."

Samantha put the box down and took a deep breath. "No it won't, because I know someone stole it."

"What do you mean, *stole* it?" Professor Caine asked curtly. "Who would do such a thing? No one can get back to these work areas unless they have a security card. Surely, you're not suggesting an employee took it."

Sam tried to phrase her answer exactly right. "I'm sure not wild about the idea of someone stealing it, especially since only *Jackson* and I were back here at the time. But we can't avoid the hard facts either – the piece was here, then it wasn't. No one moved it, misplaced it, or put it away. It had to have been stolen."

Professor Caine's tone became flinty. "That, young lady, is a very serious accusation. If I were you, I wouldn't say anything until I had solid proof to back up such an outrageous statement. We are talking about fouling the museum's credibility and ruining someone's career."

Sam gulped. "Yes sir. I realize what I'm saying. The best solution would be to find the fossil; then we might be able to track down who took it."

"This is a phantom item that doesn't show up in any documents. I know you don't want to believe it, Samantha, but I think what you saw was a piece of broken plaster that was routinely discarded by one of the technicians who know actual fossils." There was no mistaking the implication in the harsh words. "It had no identification numbers, which it most certainly would have had if it was an actual specimen, and I'm not prepared to accuse anyone on the strength of what some inexperienced teenager saw! Why the museum is part of this ridiculous work experience program, I'll never understand. From what I see," and here he shook his head, "it's not worth the aggravation."

The discussion ended abruptly as the professor turned to a leg bone and began marking it for examination. Sam continued loading her box in silence. No one could accuse the professor of being overindulgent, that was for sure. In a way, she could take it as a compliment. The professor didn't treat her any differently from the rest of his slaves and she'd heard him snap at plenty of museum staff.

Covertly keeping everything and everyone under surveillance for the remainder of the day, Sam went unrewarded as no new clues presented themselves. Her case had stalled.

Paige dropped by, and Sam called her aside. "I hope things are going better in Computerville. The atmosphere is pretty glacial here." She related Professor Caine's response when she'd suggested someone had stolen the missing fossil. "He said I should have a ton of proof to back up any accusations, so after work tonight, I'm going to hunt for the fossil. I'm one of the few people who has actually seen it."

"That could be dangerous, Sam," Paige warned nervously. "Whoever has it hidden obviously went to a lot of trouble to make it disappear without a trace. Don't forget Agent D is still prowling around."

Sam thought of the newspaper article about the guard who'd been killed at the last fossil robbery, realizing how deadly serious this had become. And she thought of the promise she'd made to her mom and dad that she would stay out of trouble while she was away. If she continued, she could be putting her life at risk. On the other hand, if she found the missing fossil, it could help the RCMP nail the culprit responsible for this *Death by Dinosaur Case,* as she'd nicknamed it.

Smiling reassuringly at her cousin, Sam said with a confidence she hoped was warranted. "No sweat. I've spent years studying how to snoop unobtrusively."

Chapter 12

DANGER IN THE DARK

The snooping unobtrusively began as soon as the day ended. Sam went to the cafeteria and dawdled over a root-beer float while she waited for the work areas to empty.

"You're too young to worry about overtime, Samantha!"

Startled, Sam nearly sneezed root beer out her nose. With a huge effort, she managed to keep it down as she turned to face kindly Dr. Beech.

"Oh, no overtime sir. I promised myself a reward for working extra hard today and this is what I picked." She held up the gloopy glass of melted ice cream and mud-coloured pop. She could tell he didn't consider the sticky beverage much of a reward.

"Don't stay too late, my dear. At your age, you shouldn't spend any more time than necessary cooped up in this dusty old bone yard. I'll be in my office for a short while if you need me."

Doctor Beech sure is nice, she thought as she watched him walk away. He was always poking around in the labs, talking to the staff and inquiring how things were going, plus he never criticized. Instead, he offered advice and knew every inch of the museum inside out. Maybe she should ask him where the best place to hide a seventy-five-million-year-old bone would be.

Dawdling without drawing suspicion was an art form, and you could only do it for so long without some helpful soul coming over to ask if everything was okay. This meant she'd need to find a safe place to wait out any staff who might be working late. She had no choice. A stint standing on a toilet seat in the ladies' washroom was required. Definitely not one of the more glamorous aspects of spying.

After an ice age of standing on her porcelain perch, Sam was sure the coast would be clear. Carefully, she made her way through the quiet, empty building to the employees' locker room. Jackson had committed the mistake of showing her how to use the locks by demonstrating on his own. Sam had filed his combination away without even thinking about it. She made sure the area was deserted then quickly moved to Jackson's locker and dialled the correct numbers. The lock clicked open obligingly.

His locker was neat without being fanatical. It contained an assortment of reference books, torn papers, old lunch bags and two battered calculators. There was also a pair of well-used hiking boots and a rock hammer painted bright purple. What was missing was a weird piece of plaster with a black X on the side.

Sam closed the door and snapped the lock shut, automatically wiping her fingerprints off the metal with her shirtsleeve. She hadn't really expected to find her prize in the first place she checked, but sometimes long shots paid off.

The next logical place was the main fossil storage area, which contained hundreds of pieces. She'd be all night if she inspected every individual bin, shelf, and cupboard. And yet, she had to try; maybe she'd get lucky.

When Sam pushed open the storage door, the room was dark, very dark...darker than the inside of a dinosaur! She fumbled with the light switch and the mercury vapour lights hummed, but the room stayed black. Then she remembered the lights took a moment to warm up. Sam waited as an eerie radiance slowly illuminated the huge room. She shivered. As soon as the lights were fully on, she made her way through the maze of storage bins.

Inspecting the aisles of neatly stacked fossils, it occurred to Sam that she might never find the missing piece. Row after row of bins, all labelled and dutifully marked, stood waiting before her. Working her way to the back section of the room, Sam worried about how much time had already gone by. She cranked her efforts up a notch. As she was about to leave the dusty corner designated for storage of the South American project, she noticed something odd. A rusty bin next to the floor had no writing on the drawer but did have a shiny new padlock run through the handle. Ah-ha!

Sam pulled on the lock without success. Her heart thumped a little faster. What would James Bond do? Probably get some new super gadget from Q that would vaporize the dumb lock with the press of a button.

That's it! *A gadget!* She needed a gadget, in this case the bolt cutters from the assembly room. They were used on the steel rods that held the skeletons together. She could cut the lock off with them! Sam hurried back down the dimly lit hallway. Her only light was that given off by the exit signs and the lit security locks on the lab doors. At the far end of the hallway, by the employee entrance, the TV screen that showed the outside of the building glowed dully above the door.

The technician who ran the fabrication room where the huge fossils were pieced together was a neat freak, which Sam was thankful for as she felt her way to the tool storage cabinet. She knew the bolt cutters would be safely put away exactly where they should be. Sam's confidence in the Obsessive Compulsive Disorder employee was rewarded as her fingers felt the long handles of the cutters. She noted the exact position so she could return them without causing any stress to the employee tomorrow.

Moments later she was back in the storage area, busily trying to gnaw the heavy lock off with the unwieldy tool. She would need a lot more strength to snip it free, or…some mechanical advantage. She laid one of the two wooden handles of the cutting jaws against the floor then wedged the jaws firmly onto the padlock. With both feet planted on that handle, she leaned her weight down on the top one. The lock snapped in two as the sharp-edged cutters sliced through the hasp like a hot knife through a Nanaimo Bar.

"Great!" Sam breathed, wiggling the broken metal off the bin. Carefully, she opened the drawer. Nestled inside, was a small piece of plaster with a telltale X clearly showing.

Eureka! She'd found the missing fossil! After all the drama around this thing, she could hardly believe her eyes.

Sam gently lifted it out. Nothing else was in the drawer – no hard evidence or even a hint as to who had stashed the fossil there. Had it been Jackson? One thing was certain. Whoever hid it would soon come for it. All she had to do was wait, watch and listen. The perpetrator was sure to give himself away with some telltale action or comment and then she'd have him. Sam tucked the troublesome specimen safely into her backpack.

Feeling quite pleased with herself for a job well done, she returned the bolt cutters and made her way through the darkened hallways toward the exit. As she passed the large foyer window, something caught her attention.

The big parking lot was empty except for one car in the far corner. Was there still someone working here? She listened to the building as it slept. All she heard were the usual mechanical noises as the automatic systems continued running the facility while no one was there, at least no one who was supposed to be there.

Quietly, Sam walked down the hallway toward the exit. She would have to use her employee card to open the door as the alarms would be turned on and she didn't need twenty overzealous policemen demanding she empty her pack.

Up ahead, the TV monitor above the exit shimmered. As she was about to pass her security card in front of the magic box, she glanced up at the eerily lit screen above her head. The picture of the outside entry area appeared as it always did. She held her card in front of the scanning device.

A bright dot on the screen drew her attention back to the monitor.

She recoiled from the card scanner as if it held a live cobra and stared at the image, trying to figure out what the tiny light in the darkness was. Then it moved and she knew. It was the lit end of a cigarette. The inky blackness surrounding the spark now took on an ominous air.

The car she'd seen in the parking lot flashed into her mind. It was blue and she remembered the blue rental car at the motel she and Paige had staked out. It had to be Agent D. He must have known from her bicycle that she was still in the building. He'd figured out what she was up to. All he had to do was wait till she left, then attack her and take the fossil.

Sam's heart pounded so loudly, she was afraid he'd hear it right through the door.

Slowly, silently, she backed away. She was out of options as her limited security card would open only one other exit – the large overhead shipping door. This would cause a lot of noise, which would certainly alert Agent D as to where she was. Sam had no choice.

The shipping door was on the other side of the building from where Agent D waited and would buy her a couple of minutes, allowing her time to get to her bicycle and freedom. There was only one teensy problem with this scenario. A bike was no match for a car. He'd be able to run her down as she tried to escape. She'd end up as prairie roadkill!

Sam threaded her way through the quiet building. The maze of corridors went on forever before she finally arrived at the receiving area and the overhead door. Taking a deep breath, she held the card in front of the scanner; her arms tingled from the tension. The massive door clicked, whirred and noisily began opening.

Sam swiped her card again causing the door to change direction and start to close, then she quickly dropped to the floor and wiggled under it. Running as fast as she could, she sprinted for her bike. She heard the door clang shut as she fumbled with the combination on her chain lock.

Her brain and fingers were having a little trouble co-ordinating their efforts, which was rather frustrating to say the least. Finally, the lock came open. She left it lying on the ground and leapt onto the bike, churning the pedals as though the devil himself were after her, which was, in fact, the case.

The sound of running feet told her Agent D had figured out what she was up to and was now closing in. Something clicked in her brain and she suddenly had a brilliant idea. Sam swung her bicycle toward the far corner of the parking lot. She needed only one small piece of luck for her idea to work.

She caught movement in her peripheral vision. The dark figure of a man raced across the parking lot toward her and she increased her speed. For an old beater, her bike really moved out!

Skidding to a stop at the car, she scanned the windows. "And we have a winner!" she crowed, dropping the bike and running to an open window on the car.

In the summer, Drumheller could reach off-the-charts temperatures, and today had been a hot one. Agent D had left the window open enough so that Sam could slide her arm in and undo the lock on the door, which she did in a heartbeat. Pulling the door open, she spied the hood release button located down by the steering column.

One of the few things she knew about cars was they had to have spark plugs to run, and where there were spark plugs, there were spark-plug wires. Flipping the release button, she ran to the hood, opened it and reached into the engine cavity. Sam pulled on the rubbery cables with all her strength and was rewarded as they popped off quite nicely. Clutching the bundle, she jumped on her bike and sped out of the lot as fast as her legs could spin the pedals.

Rounding the last corner before reaching the main road, Sam heard a very satisfying sound drifting to her on the warm evening breeze. It was the repeated whine of an unwilling engine trying to start.

Chapter 13

STASHING THE GOODS

Sam stowed her bike in the garage and went as calmly as possible into the boarding house. Everyone was enjoying a noisy game of PS4 bowling on the wide-screen TV. Sam enjoyed watching the LaSalle sisters and nodded enthusiastically as Clarisse pulled down a strike. You didn't think of 'frail' when you saw them play.

Doing a quick head count, Sam noted Jackson was nowhere to be seen, then remembered how, at coffee break, he'd mentioned something about leaving tomorrow for the weekend. *Maybe he changed his mind and left tonight,* she thought. Paige wasn't there either and Sam decided she must be waiting in their room to hear if the treasure hunt had been a success. She hurried upstairs, anxious to inspect the fossil that had caused so much trouble and show it to her cousin.

The room was empty. Sam wanted to wait but for her, waiting was impossible. Emptying her pack, she peered at the white blob of plaster lying on the bed. Looking at it now, she could hardly believe it had caused all this fuss. She picked it up. The shape was right, but it weighed a lot less than the other pieces from that portion of the shipment. It was probably due to the poor wrapping job done by the Colombian bone smuggler. Gently, she rattled the plaster-jacketed fossil.

One thing was for sure, Agent D knew she had it and would undoubtedly try to get it back. She had to put it somewhere safe. Somewhere no one, not even Jackson, who knew the boarding house, could find it.

With a bang, the door burst open, and Paige rushed into the room.

Sam squeaked loudly. It was an unprofessional but totally understandable reaction. "Holy jalapeños, Paige! You nearly gave me a double coronary!" She clutched her chest dramatically. "Come in and close the door."

Paige kicked the door shut and sat on Sam's bed. "I was in the kitchen getting a snack when I saw you slink in. Is this the famous fossil?"

"Yes. I told you I could find it." Sam leaned back on the bed, lacing her hands behind her head. "And it was no easy feat," she added, tossing out the hook, juicy bait attached.

"This is so next-level exciting! I need details." Paige was all ears. "Oh, and I made up some excuse about you working late, then going for a ride on your bike. Mrs. O'Reilly bought it, but I don't think Jack swallowed one word. He put his coat on and said he was going to the movies. Well?" She rushed on. "You didn't find this in Jack's locker, did you?"

Sam's ears perked up. "You said he went to the movies? That's odd. Yesterday, I asked Mrs. O'Reilly what was playing and she said the theatre was closed for renovations." Sam added this to her mental mix. Jackson must not know this tidbit of neighbourhood info because it blew his cover story out of the water. Was he at another mystery meeting? Or was he on his way to pick up the fossil? And when he found it gone, then what? Agent D would be able to fill him in on who got there first.

Paige jumped to Jackson's defence. "I know what you're thinking and you can cut it out. Of course, he didn't know the theatre was closed but he's not the bad guy in all this, Sam. So, tell me, was the old bone in Jack's locker?"

"Not in anyone's locker," Sam answered cryptically.

"I knew it!" Paige said smugly. "You still don't have any hard evidence against my super dude."

"All I said was I didn't find it in his locker. He could easily have been the one who stole, then stashed the thing. I'll figure it out eventually." Sam was still reluctant to drop him as her prime suspect. He and Agent D were in cahoots somehow, she was sure.

"Not gonna happen." Paige sat down on the edge of the bed. "Okay, okay, back to the museum search and I want every dusty, dirty dinosaur detail."

There was a sharp knock at the door. Startled, Sam dived for the fossil, knocking Paige off the bed and onto her butt on the floor in the process. "Quick! I'll hide the evidence!" she whispered hoarsely. "You stall them!"

"Right! I'll stall them." Paige hastily picked herself up and slammed her body against the door. "One minute," she trilled in a high, sing-song voice.

Sam hopped from her bed to Paige's in one huge leap and grabbed her cousin's Timmy Turtle pyjama bag. Yanking open the zipper, she pulled Paige's PJs out of the bag – then an old T-shirt, three dirty socks, a half-eaten jar of peanut butter and a hoodie. "Hey, it's my missing hoodie!" Sam threw the grungy pullover onto her own bed.

Grabbing the scrunched up T-shirt, she wrapped the fossil in it and stuffed it back into Timmy, then replaced him on her cousin's bed. In one deft movement, she bounded onto her own bed, grabbed a magazine and lay back as though she'd been reading for hours.

Paige opened the door and grinned idiotically.

"What are you two up to?" Rose pushed her way in.

"Us?" Sam asked innocently. "Why, nothing. Nothing at all."

"Then why are you reading your copy of *Field and Stream* upside down?" Rose asked pointedly.

"Busted," Paige giggled. "You'll have to forgive her, Rose. Sam flunked Spy Basics 101."

"So what's all the mystery about?" Rose started to sit on Paige's bed.

"No!" Sam screeched as she rolled off her own bed and grabbed the limp turtle by the neck. "Ah, I mean...please don't sit on Timmy. He doesn't enjoy being squished."

Suspicion leapt onto Rose's face. "I think you should give old Auntie Rose the full scoop. Starting with your little green buddy." She lifted her chin in Timmy's direction.

Sam knew the jig was up. She unzipped the pyjama bag. "This is the fossil everyone is smuggling, stealing, hiding, finding, chasing." She tossed the piece to Rose. "And I have a story worthy of Commander Bond about what happened while I was tracking it down." She recounted the harrowing adventure at the museum as her small audience sat speechless, listening.

When she finished, Rose stood up and paced. "This is getting dangerous. If this Agent D of yours knows where you live, he'll come here after you."

"Don't worry. I'm going to hide it. He'll never be able to find it – even with Jackson's help." Sam sat back on the bed.

Paige shot her an acid glance, which Sam ignored.

Rose shook her head. "It's still hard to believe Jackson's mixed up in this. He's always been so nice."

"He's been so *clever*," Sam corrected. "I know it's harsh, but you can't ignore all the evidence like the little ten-thousand-dollar slip and the fact I found the fossil at the museum, as I had deduced, plus, the *pièce de résistance* – he was out tonight maybe waiting to rendezvous with his accomplice, who happens to be having a little car trouble."

"You have to tell the police," Rose told Sam, her concern obvious.

"No. At least, not yet." Sam stood up. "I still don't have any concrete proof as to who stole it. I've got to have an airtight case before going to the police, or I'll be tagged as one of those crackpot teenagers we're always reading about. Maybe there's a logical explanation why Jackson's mixed up in this. Please, Rose..."

Rose considered a moment. "Oh, all right – under one condition. You must tell someone in authority about all this. It's getting dangerous."

"I will," Sam promised. "Cut my throat and hope to choke."

Paige groaned.

"For crying out loud, it's just an expression." Sam sat back down on the bed and relaxed. Everything was falling into place, sort of. "And speaking of promises, Rosie, have you asked John out yet?"

Rose blushed and quickly changed the subject. "I think I'll pop down and make us a nice cup of tea. I know I could use one."

"You can always use one," Paige added.

After Rose left, Sam retrieved the fossil and wrapped it in brown paper.

"What are you doing?" Paige watched as her cousin taped up the package.

"I'm hiding this so no one will be able to get at it," Sam explained.

"How? By disguising it in a plain brown wrapper? Why didn't I think of that?" Paige smacked her forehead. "What a great idea! Right out of the pages of *Spy Monthly*. No self-respecting crook would ever think of looking for it *wrapped*, especially when it's wrapped so tackily."

"Knock it off, Paige." Sam smoothed a section of the wrinkled paper covering the fossil, then rummaged in a drawer for a pen.

"Now what?" Paige asked. "Are you going to put a label on it that says, 'I am not a smuggled, stolen dinosaur bone. Please ignore me'?"

"Very funny," Sam retorted. "Actually, I'm going to make sure no one can find it."

Paige didn't follow her. "How? Where? There are only so many places to hide something in a boarding house."

Sam finished writing on the bundle and inspected her work. "That's right. So, it won't be in the boarding house. I'm *mailing* it to myself. It will be away for at least three days and lost deep within Canada Post." She hefted the well-taped package. "How much do you think this will cost to mail…parcel rate?"

Saturday arrived, sunny and perfect. Even though Sam felt safe with the fossil tucked in the corner mailbox, she was still going to keep her word to Rose. The question was who could she trust to tell?

The black marks in Jackson's guilty column were mounting up, and she had to do something to turn up the heat on this case. She wanted to know whether Jackson Lunde was dirty, to use a technical spy term. Hopping on her trusty bike, she rode over to Professor Caine's house.

Although the gruff man didn't have a warm fuzzy molecule in his body, he was probably her best ally. She was sure the professor would want to help solve this mystery, especially if his *protégé*, Jackson, was involved.

"What can I do for you Samantha?" Professor Caine asked after they were seated in his study.

Sam cleared her throat. "It's about the missing fossil."

"The *alleged* missing fossil," he corrected her. "We have yet to establish it was, in fact, a real fossil. No one else, except you, thinks it was."

"True," Sam took a deep breath. "The thing is, I know for a fact the piece really exists and is probably a fossil, a very valuable fossil." The professor raised his unruly eyebrows. They reminded Sam of wiry grey caterpillars inching across his brow.

"Really? How do you know that?"

"Because…" She took another steadying breath. Her voice was a fluttering bird when she spoke. "I have the missing piece."

"You have it!" He shot to his feet. "Explain yourself, young lady."

The large man towered over Sam as she shrank back into the padded wing chair. She felt those tall, dark wings enfold her like some giant leathery bat.

"I meant to say…I *had* the fossil," she stammered. "I don't have it now, I mean, I will… soon."

Professor Caine paced up and down. The ticking of the large grandfather clock in the corner seemed to grow louder and louder until the room was filled with its thundering beat.

At last he spoke. "Samantha, I'm going to take you into my confidence."

He gave her a painful smile, as though he were unused to making his lips form that particular gesture. It did little to lessen Sam's unease.

"Not forty-five minutes ago, I received a phone call from someone who wanted to know about Jackson. This…person also hinted Jackson may be involved in something illegal, something that has to do with his trip to South America." He leaned against his desk. "It may have to do with the missing piece. I want you to bring the fossil to me so I can examine it. I'll talk to Jackson and see if he is involved in anything, shall we say – shady, and if he is, perhaps I'll be able to help him."

"That might not be a good idea," Sam protested, not wanting Jackson alerted to what she suspected.

He abruptly cut her off. "First, we must return the item to the museum as quickly as possible. Even if it does turn out to be only a fragment of plaster, it is the property of the museum and its speedy recovery would be in Jackson's favour."

Sam traced a little X on the smooth leather arm of the chair. "As I said, I don't have the fossil with me. I'll have it within a day or two. Plus, there's something else you should know. Jackson recently had ten thousand dollars deposited to his bank account, and when he first spoke to me about the South American dinosaur project, he hinted he might not be around for its completion."

The professor actually winced at this. "I should speak to Jackson immediately. I think you're right Samantha; it seems he is in some kind of serious trouble." Sam could hear the regret in his voice. He probably thought of Jackson as more of a son than an assistant. "That will have to wait," she said. "He's gone away on one of his mysterious trips and isn't expected back till tomorrow evening. No one knows where to contact him." Even to Sam this sounded bad for the guy.

"Will you have the fossil by then?"

She thought of her clever hiding spot. "Not even Merlin could get it over the weekend, sir."

The professor's eyes narrowed and he folded his arms when he spoke. "I think it would be best if I confront Jackson with the missing fossil instead of you. We don't know what lengths he'd go to in order to retrieve it."

Sam thought of the falling crates and Agent D, the accomplice. Had he killed the security guard in the robbery in Ontario? Jackson was the in-house man, which made Agent D the out-house man. *Hmm*, maybe that wasn't the best way to refer to him in her report. "Perhaps you're right, Professor, especially after the brushes I've had with Agent D."

"Is that the man you saw at the museum?" The professor moved back to the chair across from Sam.

"Yes, he was there again when I *found* the fossil. Perhaps he's the one who telephoned you about Jackson. Did the man who called have an accent?"

"Accent?" Professor Caine asked, apparently unsure of what Sam meant.

"Yes, a Spanish accent," She explained.

The professor's caterpillar brows knit together as he recalled the conversation. "As a matter of fact, now that I think about it, you're right. He did speak oddly. He may have been trying to disguise an accent."

"Maybe he planned on double-crossing Jackson and taking the fossil for himself. This guy is really dangerous. Rose, a lady who lives at my boarding house, thinks I should contact the police." Sam knew if they did tell the police, it would seriously hamper her own investigation.

Professor Caine stood and started pacing again. "I think that would be premature. We don't want to tarnish the reputation of the museum by involving it unnecessarily in a scandal, and if there is any way we can save Jackson, we owe it to him to try. Up until this, this...*mistake*, he had a bright future. I had such high hopes for him." Professor Caine hesitated and then shook his head in resignation. "The police will have to be involved eventually. However, I think it would be prudent to wait until I talk to Jackson first."

"That's what I tried to tell Rose," Sam heartily agreed. "There are too many loose ends." She was glad the professor was being reasonable. Adults usually loved to call in the cops; it made them feel like good citizens.

She got up to leave. "I'll contact you if anything new develops."

"Good idea, Samantha. I'll give you my phone number at work and home; that way you can call me as soon as you have the fossil, or if anything else...*untoward* happens. I'm sure this will all be cleared up once I see that accursed piece of plaster. In the meantime, I want you to be very careful, young lady. We'll work together to get to the bottom of this."

He jotted the numbers on a piece of paper, and Sam stuffed it into the pocket of her jeans. She was sad and glad at the same time. Sad that it was looking even worse for Jackson and glad there was now a big gun on her team.

As she rode back to the boarding house, Sam couldn't seem to shake the feeling she'd put her shoes on the wrong feet. She'd missed something, something humongous. Sam replayed her conversations with Jackson in her mind, trying to find the clue she'd missed.

This spy business was more complicated than she'd imagined. There were so many details to keep straight and too many mixed-up pieces to the puzzle to get a clear picture. She hoped Professor Caine would be able to fill in the blanks when he spoke to Jackson.

Chapter 14

MAKING THE SUSPECT LIST

"Hurry up, Paige," Sam called as she and Rose headed for Mrs. O'Reilly's car early Sunday morning.

"I have to finish packing my low-fat, high-fibre, no-carb, vitamin-enriched simulated-chocolate snack," Paige yelled back from the kitchen.

After several more delays, including a search and rescue for the sunscreen, they were finally on their way. They were heading out to take pictures of the unusual rock formations called hoodoos, which were located not far from Drumheller. These tall columns of weathered sandstone had eroded in such a way as to leave boulders of a harder material precariously perched on top, and each one was a masterpiece of Mother Nature's ingenuity.

The trip was a noisy one. They took turns singing their favourite songs as Mrs. O'Reilly's borrowed car provided an odd accompaniment of clanks, rattles and rolls.

Once they arrived, all Sam could do was gawk at the bizarre geology. "This is incredible…and gravity-defying! How do they stay up there?"

"It's a spatial anomaly," Paige whispered reverently. "Must be an equalized quantum singularity with reverse polarity."

Sam saluted. "Anything you say, Dr. Spock."

This caused her cousin to sniff disdainfully. "That's MISTER Spock to you, Earthling."

The three explorers spent several hours taking pictures and exclaiming at each new example of the weathered wonders. Rose wanted photos of Canada to send back to her family in

Wales, and the surreal hoodoos provided the perfect opportunity for lots of photography.

The day was charged with a supernatural energy. The colours of the rocks were incredibly vibrant, the grass an emerald green the Wizard of Oz would have envied and the sun was a billion-candle disco ball. Even the air tasted different. The fantastic shapes of the hoodoos were wonderful to explore.

Paige entertained their little group with an involved and less-than-scientific explanation of how the colourful formations had been made and what the types of rock were.

Sam was happy to sit in the cool shade and enjoy her lunch while Paige talked. The summer air was spicy and the constant white noise of a thousand insects humming nearly lulled her to sleep.

Finally, it was time to pack up and start the drive back.

As they were heading to town, the puzzling events at the museum ran through Sam's head. "Rose," she began as she watched the spectacular scenery flash by the car window, "why do you think Jackson is innocent of the museum bone theft?"

Rose mulled this over. "I'm not sure, except I don't feel he's guilty of anything." She hurried on before Sam could object. "I know, I know, the large bank deposit. I can't explain it either. I only know that Jackson Lunde is no thief or smuggler or murderer." She paused a moment, then added, "Litterbug maybe, that's about all."

Sam decided she was right. "I've always respected gut feelings, but if it's not Jackson, then who's behind what's been happening?"

Paige's expression was a blank and Rose frowned. "Without any other clues, I couldn't say."

Sam decided to try a different approach. "Let's do this logically. If we eliminate Jackson as a prime suspect, who's left?"

"It must be someone at the museum," Paige added, joining in.

Sam ran over the list of possible suspects in her mind.

"There are about a dozen other people involved with the South American project. I guess we'd have to count you in too, Rose, since you're the import agent." The corners of her mouth curved up. "On second thought, I'll vouch for your character, which means you can be taken off our top ten hit parade. Of course, high on the list is our mystery man, Agent D. He's obviously involved from the Colombian end. Maybe he's here because Jackson, I mean, the thief, was cutting him out of the action or maybe he's made enemies at home and has come to get the precious fossil so he can sell it and start over again, here in good old Canada."

Someone else also needed to be added. Someone she hadn't even considered before. "Then there's Doctor Beech, the curator. He certainly knows about bones and which ones would be valuable. Also, he has access to anything he wants in the museum and knows every millimetre of the joint." Another thought occurred to her. "And he works strange hours so he could do stuff without folks noticing."

Sam remembered bumping into the curator outside the uncrating room the day the fossil had gone missing and he'd been working late the night she'd found the fossil. Why hadn't she remembered those two little nuggets before? But the dear old gentleman didn't make her weirdometer so much as hum one note. There had to be someone else, someone hiding in plain sight.

Then, it hit her. "Creepy crawlers! I may have messed up big time. There's one other person who should be on the list. He's been in on this from the beginning. He sent Jackson to Colombia, and he was there when we unpacked the vertebrae box so he knew where the X piece should have been. But he didn't have enough time to find it before he was called away." She was thinking out loud and it all made terrible sense. "It could easily be Professor Caine!"

"You're right, Sam," Rose said. "But if it is, you end up back at the same question – why? What would he have to gain by smuggling an extra fossil in the shipment?"

"Let's work on one problem at a time. First, let's be sure who arranged for the dumb spare bone to be sent here, and then we'll figure out why." Sam was rapidly running over everything in her head.

"Then you admit you were wrong about Jack." Paige's tone shouted victory.

"I'm not saying Jackson isn't mixed up in this, Paige," Sam answered cautiously. "I simply want to know more about Professor Caine's involvement."

"I can't see a man of Professor Caine's reputation doing anything illegal," Rose interrupted. "He practically wrote the book on some of those dinosaurs, didn't he?"

"He's the go-to guy when it comes to these bones and he's well known," Sam agreed. "Logically, he'd have nothing to gain and everything to lose if he were mixed up in the theft. If this dinosaur is the missing link, it will put him back at the top of his game. He'd be paid more, he could go on lecture tours, make a National Geographic documentary. Who knows where this could lead!" She thought a moment. "You know what would be really helpful?"

Paige held up her fingers and made a sign to ward off evil. "Uh-oh. We're about to be snookered, Rose."

Sam ignored this. "Don't be so negative. You want to try to clear Jackson, don't you?"

"He wouldn't have to be *cleared* in the first place if you hadn't pointed out all those dumb things that make him seem, well, for want of a better description, *a low-down, bone-thieving scumbag*."

"Then here's your chance to vindicate your hero. We have to get into the museum and use the computer." Sam could feel her weirdometer tingling. She had the ingredients for a devilishly clever plan.

"Sam, even though it's Sunday, the museum is open with lots of witnesses around," Rose said hesitantly. "Crikey! Now you've got me doing it! People, *people* around!"

"Not now. It's after six, the museum is closed. No one will be there." Sam sounded extremely confident. "Paige, do you remember when I asked if you could tap into other records from your terminal? We need to access personnel files. How about it?"

"Sam, it's not only a bad idea, it's an *illegal* one." Paige shook her head, making her ponytail fly around like rust-coloured rain.

"I know it's pushing things, Paige. But I promise, this time it's important. I need to know more about Jackson and Professor Caine. Maybe a clue will turn up to help me figure this case out."

Something exploded in Paige. "I told you, *Jack's innocent!*"

Paige was angry, about as angry as Sam had seen her since they were five and there'd been that unfortunate mishap in the sandbox with the cat pee.

"Relax, Paige." Rose jumped in to calm things down. "All Sam wants to do is try to prove it."

The ride became very quiet.

Paige reluctantly gave in. "If you think it will put Jack in the clear, then yeah, sure."

"Great!" Sam said, relieved. "Let's go, Rosie."

Taking a series of back roads to ensure no one saw them going to the museum, they finally arrived in the empty parking lot.

"I've got my security card." Sam climbed out of the ancient jalopy.

"This ain't gonna be good," Paige muttered as she and Rose followed.

Sam passed her card in front of the scanning device and the door obediently clicked open.

"Can we do this from your terminal, Paige?" Sam asked as they hurried down the quiet hallways to the computer transcription room.

"Sure, it's all one system with different access codes and passwords. Speaking of codes, Sam, I did manage to come up with a few, none are for personnel though."

"We'll try what you've got." Sam held the door to the transcription room open.

Sliding past her cousin, Paige moved to her terminal. "I put the codes in a safe spot." She dropped her purse on the floor and energetically rummaged through a cluttered drawer in an extremely messy desk.

"How do you work with all that junk everywhere?" Amazed, Sam watched Paige pull a wide assortment of articles from the drawer: two thick romance paperbacks, a cardboard tube of potato chips, pens, a partially eaten chocolate bar, one cup (cracked), a transparent plastic makeup bag with several containers of potions tucked inside and one neon-pink hairbrush.

"Camouflage." Paige grabbed the makeup bag. "There it is. You see, Sam, I can get into this spy stuff too." She retrieved the brightly coloured hairbrush. It was the type that held water in the handle.

Sam reached for the brush. "In the H2O reservoir, I presume." She unscrewed the end and pulled a small cylinder of paper from inside. "Brilliant, Watson!"

"Elementary, my dear Holmes," Paige giggled.

Sam scanned the sheet. "You're right. Nothing remotely connected with what I want." She reread the list. "Punch up the personnel files anyway, and we'll see how far we get with these."

Paige switched on her terminal and waited for it to boot up. Her fingers flashed over the keys. "It says *Authorized Personnel Only! Please key in user ID and password.*"

Sam sighed, disappointed. "You can relax, cousin. I'm

thinking we may not get a chance to do anything illegal." She sat on the corner of the desk thinking. "Paige, how good is your memory?"

Paige made a pained face. "You know my lousy memory is my one flaw. Why?"

"Because I think you're not alone." Sam jerked her thumb toward the door. "Let's go to the personnel department. I have a hunch to put to the test."

All three headed down the hall to the administration section. The doors to personnel were locked with the secretary's desk sitting tidily to one side.

"Here goes," Sam muttered under her breath and walked over to the secretary's desk. "I have a great memory." She lifted various items and inspected them. "Most people, however, have memories like yours, Paige, so…" She raised the edge of the blotter on the desk. "They write things down."

Sam scribbled something on a scrap of paper. "I figured the personnel secretary would need to access security files once in a while, which would mean having a user ID of her own or using someone else's. Anything that critical would need to be either committed to memory or, written down and hidden somewhere, say…under a blotter." She held up the piece of paper, "Gotta love human frailties!"

Once back at Paige's terminal, Sam gave her the paper. "Shall we get started?"

"Easy for you to say," Paige keyed in the correct number and password. "Your incriminating fingerprints aren't all over this illegally used terminal."

"Paige, it's *your* terminal. Who else's fingerprints would be on it? What have you got?" Sam scanned the screen. The display listed different sections that could be accessed. "Let's try *Employee Resumés*. It should give us some background for both Jackson and Professor Caine."

Paige hit a few more keys. "It's asking for an employee's

name. Let's do Jack first." She typed his name into the machine.

Sam read the lengthy report. "Wow, for someone who hasn't even finished his degree yet, Jackson has already accumulated some impressive credentials. He spent the last three summers working as an assistant for any professor even remotely connected with South American dinosaurs." She frowned as she read on. "Those assistant jobs must pay better than I thought. His work history excluding them is really sketchy and I know going to university is very expensive. I wonder how he affords it?"

She finished reading his file. "It appears all his time for the past three years is accounted for." She shook her head. "Let's see what Professor Caine's been up to."

Again, Paige worked her computer magic and the machine obligingly displayed the professor's resumé. Sam read the professor's impressive list of credentials. "He must be an authority on every type of dinosaur ever born."

She hesitated, rereading the screen. "He published not only prolifically, but consistently, even when he was a student. Then five years ago, no new publications. Not a paragraph. That's kinda strange. Keep scrolling. I want to see previous employers."

Sam stared at the screen. "Nothing. There are no previous employers listed at all. He's been working at the museum for two months, but for the past five years, the professor's been off the radar. It says he got his mail from General Delivery, Medellin, Colombia, with no residence or business address given."

Rose shook her head sympathetically. "It seems the professor has been homeless for five years in Colombia."

"Poor guy," Sam agreed. "Down and out in some tropical jungle, sweltering and wasting away while he searched for the elusive *Pachycephalosaurus*."

Rose and Paige both looked at her like she'd said something

unsuitable for polite company.

Sam ignored them. "It explains why he came back to Canada for a job. Doctor Beech was doing a favour for a brilliant scientific colleague and old friend, who was five years out of touch." She considered this latest twist. "He turned himself around and now he's obviously back into his work. The South American project shows he still knows his field, inside and out."

Sam listed the information they'd gained. "Jackson has a background that is financially unstable and points to ten thousand dollars as a strong motive for bone theft, and from his past work experience, I'd say he's got a real thing for South American dinos. Professor Caine has a background that is blank and probably grim. He was homeless and dino obsessed and is now working at regaining his former glory in a field he practically invented. But would he gamble his reclaimed professional respect by risking being caught as a thief, even if the bone turned out to be the valuable missing link he could sell to some private collector or a museum? Something doesn't make sense. What we need to find out is which one of them is willing to go to what lengths to have the fossil."

"So, instantly, Jack is a competitor for Crook of the Year," Paige said with only a trace of acid. "Nice. I spent all those sleepless nights worrying about the guy because you were so sure he was the *perp* – your word, not mine – and now we have contestant number two, running neck and neck."

"How are you going to find which one did it?" Rose asked.

"Easy," Sam explained. "I'm expecting a special parcel post package tomorrow. With my bait, I should be able to come up with a plan to prove who's at the bottom of this."

"What if it's Jackson?" Rose asked worriedly. "If you tell him you know he's the thief, he might do something…" She paused, searching for the right word. "…*unfortunate* and take the fossil from you."

"If you mean he might bundle me in a sack and bury me out back, let me worry about that, Rose," Sam said confidently, sure Jackson would never do anything to harm her. Then hesitated remembering the stabbed guard and the stack of crates that nearly crushed her. She also recalled how Jackson was gone and then reappeared two seconds after the accident. It was worth considering. "First I have to figure out the basic game plan, and then I'll work on the details."

"I'm still concerned it could get nasty," Rose cautioned.

"Don't worry Rosie, I'll take every precaution." Sam waited a nanosecond before continuing. "So it's all settled. My package should be delivered tomorrow and we can put *Operation Dino* into action after work."

As they left the museum and headed for the boarding house, Sam watched the sun sink below the edge of the world. The sky was an iridescent pink with shades of coral, orange and lavender. If she were right, tomorrow all the mystery surrounding the fossil would finally be solved.

She didn't want to think what would happen if she were wrong about the whole thing and this was simply a string of odd coincidences with a chunk of useless plaster at the end of it. She'd done such a good job convincing Paige and Rose, even she believed this was all real. Then again, she had to; her dreams depended on it.

Chapter 15

OPERATION DINO

The morning sun was laser bright, waking Sam way too early. With a groan, she rolled out of bed and dragged herself to the window. She had to admit, with everything so fresh and green and sparkling with dew, it was inviting. Sam yawned and stretched. Morning had always been her favourite time of day. Too bad it came so darn early.

A movement beside the tree across the street made her jump, but when she tried to see into the shadows, there was no one there. Even though the sun was already quite warm, Sam felt a chill. She hoped it was only the early light playing tricks on her overeager imagination.

One thing was for sure, she was very glad the mystery of the disappearing fossil would be solved tonight. She liked the intrigue of spying; she didn't like being the one spied upon.

At the breakfast table, Jackson plunked down next to Sam. His tangy lime aftershave wafted to her and she sniffed the light scent approvingly.

"What's new?" He reached for a slice of toast. "Anything you want to tell me?"

Sam choked on her tea. "What? No, why do you ask?" She was sure her nervousness was written in neon-red crayon across her cheeks.

"Don't be so defensive, Gopher." Jackson laughed. "I only asked because I've been away all weekend and thought you'd have dug up something exciting."

The tension leaked out of her. "*Dug up!* Ha ha. Good one from a palaeontologist. As a matter of fact, Rose, Paige and I went to the hoodoos this weekend." She kept her tone light, want-ing Jackson to think everything was normal, or as normal as it could be, considering what was going on. "We climbed around for hours and Paige ate more than her share of lunch. Oh! And Rose took a ton of pictures. She'd probably love to show you."

"It sounds like a lot more fun than I had."

Jackson's cryptic words had Sam wondering about his weekend, and early-morning meetings and a million other un-explained details that kept nudging Mr. Lunde to the top of her suspect list. She refocused. "Rose says the snaps will be a nice way to remember part of our summer so she's putting them on a flash drive for Paige and me. Speaking of remembering the summer…" She reached for more sugar for her tea. "I suppose you're hoping for a promotion if the South American dino turns out to be the missing link?"

"That's a long way in the future. Who knows, I may not even be here then. I might be fired for letting the new gopher lose important fossils." He winked at her and continued stirring his coffee.

Sam knew he was teasing, but his reference to leaving may not have been a joke. "So you admit it was a real fossil I lost, I mean, I saw?" Jackson stilled and it occurred to Sam pushing the matter might be dangerous if he really was her man. Backpedalling, she quickly changed her approach. "Actually, I'm sure you were right and it was only a chunk of plaster. I admit my imagination sometimes runs away with me. Ask any-one, and they'll tell you I'm a bit of a flake when it comes to weaving a mystery out of thin air."

She energetically buttered a piece of toast. If Jackson had hidden the fossil at the museum, he'd find out it was gone as soon as he went in today, and she didn't want to be the first person who came to mind when he searched for it. Changing the subject entirely was the wisest move. "How was your trip to Calgary?"

"How did you know I went to Calgary this weekend?" he asked sharply.

"I don't know, I guess I heard it somewhere." She was certainly having trouble saying the right thing. Sam moved back to safer ground. "Things were pretty quiet around here this weekend. You didn't miss much."

"Truth be told, I would rather have stayed here and relaxed."

"You sure spend a lot of time there. Have you got a secret girlfriend in the city?" Sam blurted.

Jackson laughed. "Nope, I only wish it was something so pleasant." He stood up abruptly. "Got to run, Gopher. I have some things to do at work. See you there."

He left her wondering about what he did in Calgary that wasn't very pleasant. Sam's attention refocused as Danny Flannigan escorted Rose and Paige into the dining room. All three were laughing. "You're all in a good mood today," Sam observed as she poured a round of tea.

"It's because Danny has some really great news" Paige explained. "Fancy-schmancy television people contacted him this weekend. They want to do a documentary about Canada's entertainment roots and he's going to be in it. Isn't it fantastic?"

"Really? Danny, you're going to be famous – again. That's so cool." Sam was genuinely happy to hear this latest news about another of the boarding-house guests.

Danny shook his head. "I don't know about famous. I will get to do my routine again and it's going to be a bit of a reunion. All the old-timers those television folks can get hold of will be there. I'm thinking of asking Marie to accompany me to Toronto for the taping."

"I think she'd love that," Sam said reassuringly.

"Morning all," John greeted them as he came into the room.

Hastily, Paige related the good news.

Sam nudged her cousin. "Gee, John, you're looking particularly dapper this morning. Rose, don't you think John is dapper?"

Rose sent a silencing message to Sam over her teacup. "Yes, John is very smartly dressed today."

"In fact," Paige added, "you could say John is positively *handsome*. Don't you agree Rose?"

Rose had turned as pink as the flowers on her teacup. "Yes, I think John is very handsome." She set her cup down a smidge too hard.

"And John…" Sam's voice was uber sweet. "Wouldn't you say Rose is lovely today?"

John was a little lost in the conversation. "Ah, I've always thought Rose was pretty. In fact…" His voice trailed off as his eyes locked with Rose's. "I think she's *very* pretty."

Sam dusted imaginary toast crumbs off her hands. "Well, now that's settled, I guess we should be heading for work. My dear Paige, shall we leave?"

Sam's accomplice jumped to her feet. "After you, my dear Samantha." She bowed and swept her fork in the direction of the kitchen door.

"No, no, my dear cousin, after you." Sam pushed the door open and ushered Paige through it.

"Why thank you, Samantha…*dear*."

They waited till the door had closed before both girls burst into laughter. "Do you think we were too subtle?" Sam asked, once they'd calmed down.

"Totally! In fact, *tact* is our middle name," Paige said.

Sam pushed her hair back from her face. "There were so many *dears* flying around in there, I was starting to think we'd have to call animal control."

This was too much for Paige and she burst out with a braying laugh any donkey would have been proud of. Both girls were still in high spirits as they left for work

◎

Finalizing details in her mind as she bicycled, Sam decided the time was right to let Paige in on the plan. "I figured out how to implement Operation Dino."

"Great. I can hardly wait for you to prove Jack's innocent." Paige pedalled faster.

Sam sped up beside her cousin. "How about this? When we get the fossil back, I'll call Professor Caine and tell him I've changed my mind about giving him the bone. I'll say I think the police should be called, and I've put it in my locker at work so I can turn it over to Dr. Beech in the morning."

"Okay." Paige urged her bicycle harder, her feet flying. "What about Jack?"

"That's where you come in." Sam gritted her teeth as she tried to stay up with her record-setting cousin. "I'll leave with the fossil so you can honestly say you don't know *exactly* where it is, and then you tell Jackson I plan to stash it in my locker in order to give it to Dr. Beech. I'll hide outside the museum and see who shows up to re-steal the old bone."

"You're sure there's no danger?" Paige asked hesitantly, slowing her frantic pace.

"Not with my ingenious plan. You're the only one who'll know I'm still at the museum. The real guilty culprit will think I've already put the fossil in safe storage and left." Sam gratefully eased up, her legs burning from the exertion.

"Sounds okay, Sam, as long as you're sure you'll be all right." Paige hiccupped nervously as she coasted into the parking lot at the museum.

"It'll be a piece of cake. With the positive ID, I'll be able to go to the police and they can take over." Sam felt good about her plan. It was a winner. Still she'd better stay clear of both Professor Caine and Jackson to avoid answering too many questions. She hoped Canada Post would hold up their end and she'd have a parcel waiting when she returned to the boarding house after work. If her planets aligned the way she hoped, she'd have all the answers tonight.

At the museum, Sam quietly made her way to the storage area where she could spend the day putting away boxes of sorted bones. Unfortunately, her plan fell through when Professor Caine sent for her to join him in the Fine Preparation Lab.

"Samantha, I have something new for you today," he explained. "You're going to learn what happens to the fossils after they've been brought in from the field and their jackets and excess matrix have been removed." Even though the fossil he gave her was still encased in a thin layer of rock, its true shape was easy to see. "You're going to carefully remove this specimen from its remaining rock matrix using these tools." He indicated an array of implements.

Sam picked up a small tool. "Is this a dentist's drill?" She pressed the trigger until it shrilled with a high-pitched whine.

"It's called an *airscribe* and it's similar, although this tool vibrates like a jack hammer and uses pressurized air to function." Professor Caine indicated an array of small picks. "These will be very familiar also. When the fossil is freed of excess material, the cleaning will be finished using *air-abrasion* which is ultra-delicate sandblasting."

"It sounds awfully slow." Sam thought of all the bones they'd unpacked for a single dinosaur.

"It is, however in this case, you don't have to remove all the matrix, so there's no worry about damaging the fossil. This bone is of interest for research and won't be on display. Lots to do so you'd better get started." He turned and left her with the fossil and the airscribe.

"Right. *Fossil Freeing – A Beginner's Guide*, here I come." Sam set to work carefully removing the outer rock from the bone, which was obviously some poor creature's rib. After two hours of painstaking work, she understood what a slow process it really was. Although the job was interesting, having Professor Caine hover over her made her wonder if he was watching out for her, or plain old watching her. He was never far away.

By the end of the day, she could almost feel the tension as the professor packed up the tools and equipment. She wasn't surprised when he called her over.

"You haven't mentioned the missing fossil, Samantha. I was wondering if you've retrieved it yet." He put the last of the tools away.

Sam took off her lab coat and hung it on a hook. "Actually, Professor, I'm hoping to get it within the next couple of days. I'll call as soon as it shows up."

"I'm glad to hear that, Samantha. If this turns out the way we think and there is a real fossil in the plaster, Jackson will be in a lot of trouble. I would hate to see his career ruined, let alone think about the possibility of his ending up in jail. He's my shining star and I hope he'll take over for me in the future."

He was so genuine in his worry about Jackson, that Sam wondered if he truly was a good guy. Picking up her backpack, she quickly headed for the computer room. Paige was waiting when she arrived.

"Did Professor Caine or Jack act very suspicious today?"

Her tone had a hint of nervousness, or was it excitement? Sam played it cool, knowing that accusing Jackson could set her cousin off. "As a matter of fact, I hardly saw Jackson. I worked with Professor Caine all day. He showed me how to clean the fossilized bones. I'm sure the specimens I work on are not the critically important one-of-a-kind variety. More likely the thousands-of-these-need-to-be-cleaned-by-some-gopher kind." Her eyes swept the room furtively. "He also asked if I had the you-know-what yet."

"What did you tell him?" Paige's voice was hushed and breathless. "You couldn't very well say the fate of the world hangs on the efficiency of Canada Post."

"I told him I'd let him know. Speaking of which, let's get going. I've got a feeling there's a parcel with my name on it waiting at Mrs. O'Reilly's."

They hurried back to the boarding house and were barely through the door when Mrs. O'Reilly called from the kitchen. "Is that you girls? Samantha, a package came for you today. Odd thing. It's on the sideboard in the front hall. Oh! And your mother called. I told her you were both doing fine."

They ran to the hall. There, innocently sitting on the old wooden cupboard, was the awkwardly taped package. The fossil in its plain brown wrapper. Sam felt relieved; now the plan could proceed. "I'll hide it in the bottom of my pack and take it with me to the Tyrrell," she said. "Then when you tell Jackson it's at the museum, you won't really be telling a lie. That way, if he's the one, he won't tear up the boarding house to find it."

"He's so not the one and he's certainly not going to flip out and go psycho on me." Paige huffed and folded her arms defensively.

"Okay, chill. One more 'Health and Safety' thing – I need you to promise Rose is with you when you tell him. If he does react…" she hesitated, "*badly,* you might need the help."

"Gee, thanks," Paige said sarcastically. "It's nice to know you're always thinking of my safety first, or at least second." She headed for the kitchen to help with supper.

Jackson was strangely quiet during the evening meal, which suited Sam. She didn't want to make small talk. But did his silence mean he was her man and he'd discovered the fossil was missing? Her stomach tied itself into complicated knots. As soon as they'd finished clearing away the dinner dishes, Sam signalled Paige. *Operation Dino* was about to commence.

Sam slipped up to her room and changed into her black jeans and turtleneck. If she was going to be hiding in the bushes, she wanted to be dressed for it. The scrap of paper with the phone number Professor Caine had given her was on the table in her room. She grabbed it and headed downstairs. Taking a deep breath, Sam picked up the receiver on the old-fashioned phone. As she dialled, she frowned. Something nagged at the back of her brain.

"Hello?"

Sam cleared her throat. "Professor Caine, this is Samantha Stellar. I called to tell you the fossil came today."

"That is good news, Samantha."

His voice was friendly and Sam found herself relaxing slightly.

"Why don't you bring it over to my house?"

"Actually, Professor, I've decided to turn the bone over to Doctor Beech in the morning. I feel there have been too many strange things happening around the fossil." She held her breath.

"I agree Doctor Beech should be brought in on this. Right now, I'm still hoping we can help Jackson out of this mess. We don't even know it's actually a fossil. Once I examine it to make sure it's authentic, I might be able to convince Jackson to explain why he took it and try to set things right. It would go much easier for him." He waited for her to say something.

She tried not to think about how much sense this made; instead, Sam gritted her teeth. "No, I'm not going to do that. The fossil is in my locker at the museum. It will be safe there until morning when the authorities can have it. I'll see you tomorrow, Professor Caine."

She hung up quickly, not waiting for his reply. Her heart was pounding hard. Back in her room, she dropped the paper onto her night table, noticing her hands were trembling – verging on shaking. Not professional at all. When she went into this spy business full-time, she was going to need a lot of stress management. Grabbing her backpack, Sam quietly left the boarding house.

Paige was waiting for her in the garage. "Sam, I'm kind of scared." The worry in her voice was genuine. "Before, it was all a game. Nothing ever happened with all your other adventures, but this time it's different. This is real."

Sam saw that her cousin was frightened. "Don't worry. Rose is here so you won't be alone, and all I'm going to do is watch from the bushes to see who shows up. I'll be back before you know it." Sam finished tugging on her pack. "Give me a twenty-minute head start before you tell Jackson about the old bone. It will give me time to set up my stakeout." She gave Paige the thumbs-up and climbed on her bicycle.

The light was failing rapidly as Sam stashed her bike in a clump of bushes at the far end of the parking lot. There were no cars, and she couldn't see any lights on in the building. Good, she'd beat the thief here. Settling in behind the cotoneaster hedge, Sam made sure she had a clear view of both the main and staff entrances. She didn't know how long she'd have to wait and hoped it would all be over soon.

Time crawled painfully by and her legs were cramped from the prolonged stint in the bushes when she thought she heard a noise behind her.

With lightning speed, a black gloved hand clamped tightly over her mouth! Panic seized her as she felt herself being dragged farther back into the bushes.

Sam tried to scream. She clawed at the vice-tight arms holding her. Twisting, she turned to see who'd grabbed her, but the iron grip forced her head down, squeezing her windpipe. Her mind raced as she struggled to take in oxygen.

Suddenly, Sam saw a blinding flash. The dying rays of the sun glinted ominously off a polished steel blade! He had a knife! *A knife!*

The previous summer she'd taken a self-defence course. Frantically, she tried to recall the basic techniques she'd been taught. From the corner of her eye, she spied her assailant's foot; then, using all her strength, she smashed her heel onto his instep. He cried out in pain and Sam felt the grip loosen. She quickly drove her elbows into his ribs...one, two. The lethal hold faltered.

Seizing her chance, Sam bolted for the building. Ice slid down her spine as she remembered seeing black gloves like those before! With horror, she realized she'd made a fatal mistake. She hadn't accounted for everyone involved. She hadn't accounted for the one person who had started this all in the first place. Agent D!

If she could make it into the building, she'd be safe. As far as she knew, Agent D didn't have a security card to open any of the doors.

Her legs burned from the exertion, and all she could hear was the blood pounding in her ears. Panting, she reached the employee entrance. As she fumbled in her pockets for the magic card, footsteps pounded behind her. Pulling a comb out of her pocket, she dropped it to the ground; a package of gum was next, followed by a wad of scrunched-up bills – the remains of her paycheque.

Her fingers touched the card, and relief flooded through her. With shaking hands, she held the plastic key card up to the scanner, praying the machine would read the code quickly. Mercifully, the lock clicked and Sam pulled the door open. Slamming it closed behind her, she stumbled down the darkened hallway.

Her breath came in raspy gasps. She tried to calm her breathing and told herself she was safe, she was safe, *she was safe!* The adrenaline in her system started to wear off and she slumped against the wall, then slid wearily down to the floor. She was safe.

Taking a deep breath, she tried to slow her pounding heart. Agent D couldn't get her in here and – she relaxed as she felt the pack against her back – he couldn't get the fossil either. How had he found out she was at the museum? Either the professor or Jackson must have called and told him she'd be here. She'd made a foolish, and almost fatal, mistake.

Sam thought back to the harrowing attack. With a tingling buzz, her weirdometer spiked, sending prickles coursing through her entire body.

She hadn't actually seen her assailant's face and anyone can wear black gloves...

Panic twisted her stomach again. *Don't do it. The monster under the bed can't get you if you don't look.* She glanced back at the door.

Then she heard it.

The unmistakable clicking sound of a lock being released. Her heart slammed in her chest and her throat tightened, choking off a scream.

The door slowly opened. There, silhouetted against the evening sky, was a dark figure, and he was holding the deadly blade.

Chapter 16

DEATH AND DINOS

As Sam scrambled to her feet, the setting sun lanced through the open doorway and directly into her eyes, blinding her. Blinking to clear her vision, she tried to see the man's face but it was no good. He was a dark wraith surrounded by fiery light.

Frantically, Sam searched for a way to escape. Her only option was to go farther into the building. She bolted down the corridor desperately trying to think of a plan as she rattled doorknobs along her way. The doors were all locked and unfortunately, her magic card only worked on certain doors in selected areas. Apparently, the doors in this area weren't on that list.

If only she could come up with a plan to immobilize the creep. The trouble was, she didn't have a lot of time to set a trap. She knew her card would work on the Preparation Room and sprinted through the corridors toward her goal. Holding the card up to the scanner, she heard the welcoming click and pushed the door open. Quickly scanning the dimly lit space, she searched for anything she might use as a weapon. The room was pristine.

On the stainless steel table was a huge leg bone being readied for display. The sling used to move the unwieldy bone hung loosely beside the table. It was attached to a large overhead winch. If she were Fred Flintstone, she'd pick it up and crack the thug over the head.

In a desperate flash, an idea came to her. Hurrying to the sling, she pulled it toward the bone.

Sliding a section of the canvas carrier under each end of the huge fossil, she ran for the electric control. Flicking the switch, she hoped the whirring sound meant the bone was being lifted. The cable connected to the sling snapped taut. "Score!" she crowed as the bone rose slowly into the air.

When it was chest high, Sam halted the winch. Grabbing a length of rope from a workbench, she tied one end to the sling and the other end she passed behind a support pillar, then pulled with all her strength. The sling groaned as the massive bone inched backward.

Just as she thought she could hold the rope no longer, the door burst open. She let go and the sling, with its heavy cargo cradled in the canvas folds, arced toward the door.

Before the shadowy figure could react, the huge battering ram slammed into him. The force of the impact sent him back, out of the room, to collide heavily with the wall in the hallway.

Sam didn't wait to see if he was dead or only stunned. She ran out of the room and away from the still, silent figure on the floor.

Reaching the end of the hall, she desperately pulled on the heavy door. It led to the front entry and freedom. But the door wouldn't open! For security reasons, it was kept locked to seal off the work section of the museum from the front galleries.

Her security card! Her magic card would open the door. She reached into her back pocket. *It was gone.* She must have dropped it...back there. Sam turned to the prone figure still sprawled face down on the floor. He hadn't moved. Maybe she'd killed him.

Cautiously, she edged back down the hall toward the dark prep room.

The figure didn't move.

She spotted the missing key card. It was lying beside the body. Warily, she reached slowly out and picked it up.

Curiosity had always been bad for cats, and Sam was no feline. But she just had to know who the guy was. Turning to the body, she listened for any sign of life. No ragged breathing... no faint moan of pain... The only sound in the still hallway was her own heart pounding in her ears. Cautiously, she reached out to remove the hat covering the man's head.

As fast as a striking snake, his hand shot out and encircled her ankle in that now familiar iron grip.

Sam screamed and tried to pull her foot free, but it was no use. Using her best street fighting form, she kicked as hard as she could with her other foot. There was the sickening sound of a bone snapping, and she was released.

Her assailant shrieked in pain, lunging for her with his other hand. Sam seized her millisecond and bolted. She held her card up to the first scanner she came to and pulled on the doorknob. The door swung open, and she fled through it, pulling it shut behind her.

Sam found herself in the gigantic dinosaur exhibition hall where fossilized skeletons were displayed. It was more than a little eerie to creep through the dark, cavernous room. The huge creatures stared down at her with empty eye sockets as she silently moved among them.

Some were stark fossilized bones, white and bare. Others, lifelike mock-ups with skin and claws and razor-sharp teeth. It was deathly quiet and gave a whole new meaning to *silent as the grave*. She really was walking through a seventy-five-million-year-old tomb.

An ominous click of the locking mechanism on the gallery door warned her she was not out of danger yet. Trying not to trip in the gloom, she rushed to the nearest exit and held her card up to the scanner. Nothing happened. Her card wouldn't work on the exit door. She was trapped!

Sam ran back to one particularly frightening display in which the towering skeleton of an *Albertosaurus* stood gloating over its kill, the barrel-shaped carcass of a *Stegosaurus*.

Hurrying to the unfortunate beast, Sam dropped down

onto the sand and, as quickly as possible, crawled inside the large rib-cage cavity. As she scuttled forward, her glasses fell into the sand and disappeared.

Sam peered blurrily through the bars of her bizarre sanctuary. This wouldn't do. If her pursuer found her now, she'd be blind and helpless. She had to be able to see whoever was after her.

Running her hands through the sand, she felt for her glasses. "Success!" she whispered, grabbing her specs and shoving them back on. They were dusty and scratched, but in one piece. Above her the huge skull of the *Albertosaurus* leered down. *My, what big teeth you have, Grandma!* She shook her head; the stress was getting to her.

Listening intently, Sam tried to determine where her assailant was. She prayed whoever was stalking her would pass right by in the darkened room. Her heart skipped a beat when the trench-coated figure stopped in front of the display where she was hiding.

"You may as well come out, Samantha. I've sealed all the outside exits. Your card won't work on them. I'm going to find you."

Sam gulped. She'd know that voice anywhere.

Chapter 17

UNMASKED!

It was Professor Caine!

Sam's mouth went dry as her gaze was drawn to the deadly knife in his hand.

"All I want is the fossil. I won't hurt you."

Fat chance, thought Sam, as she watched him walk toward the wall at the far end of the gallery. She heard the snap of the main lighting switches. With a familiar hum the warming mercury vapour lights threw a faint glow. She had mere seconds before the entire exhibition hall was flooded in cold, hard light.

Sam eased out of the skeleton and, gauging the distance, bolted for the door back to the work areas. This time the magic card was out before she was even near the scanner. She hit the door running, her shoulder solidly smacking the heavy door, forcing it open.

The door flew back, taking Sam with it. She nearly fell as the knob wedged itself into the wall. The force of the impact jarred her security card out of her grip, but the sound of heavy steps approaching didn't allow her time to search for it.

This is bad; this is really bad, Sam thought, as she rocketed down the dark corridor. She could hear the professor behind her. Escape was impossible!

The only door left open was the one to the Noxious Laboratory. She remembered it had windows to the outside. Maybe she could break one and escape.

There was no point trying to hide her movements now. Racing into the room, she flipped on the lights to save precious seconds as she searched for some tool to smash the window.

Quickly, she surveyed the room. Great! There wasn't a chair or stool in the place. Pulling open drawers, Sam hoped to find a hammer or at least a piece of pipe. Nothing. Why were these people such neat freaks? Couldn't they have left a convenient taser out on the bench in case some sweet, teenaged girl needed to save herself from a homicidal maniac?

"You seem to have run out of places to hide, Samantha." Professor Caine stood in the doorway, one arm hanging limply at his side. "It wouldn't have done any good to try and break the glass. It's specially reinforced – what you'd call *unbreakable*."

"Think of what you're doing, Professor." Sam's voice was weak in her dry throat."

"Oh, I am, my dear. I've been working on this *project* for the last five years, while I rotted in Bellavista Prison, just outside my favourite holiday destination, sunny Medellin." His face twisted into a gargoyle's mask. "The only good thing about that Colombian hellhole was my incarceration put me in touch with the contacts who would assist me in becoming a wealthy man! Back in Canada, I spent months pretending to be a delivery driver or a technician or even a lost tourist, which allowed me to get into other museums and steal legitimate pieces. I knew this would ensure no one would worry too much when one small fossil disappeared from this shipment." His voice rose to a roar. *"Then you come along and almost ruin my whole plan!"*

Sam stalled for more time. Right now, her life expectancy was counted in seconds, and she wanted every one of those seconds. "You killed a guard at the last museum."

The professor seemed genuinely pained. "It was an accident. I was leaving with the fossil when the guard found me. He thought I was a weak old man. The poor fool soon found out what years of hard physical labour in prison can do for one's muscles. We wrestled, I pushed him and the clumsy oaf fell." He shrugged his good shoulder. "Unfortunately, there was a *Triceratops* model behind him and he impaled himself. Tragic really – still, not my fault."

Sam didn't point out that if he hadn't been stealing in the first place, the guard would never have tackled him. Professor Caine was insane. This fact became even more obvious as he continued laying out her short future.

"You're going to have a little accident too." His face twisted in rage. "That stack of crates should have finished you off. You have an aggravating way of avoiding death, Samantha Stellar. This time I won't miss. The headlines will read about the tragic death of a young girl in an attack by an unknown assailant. Her dead body found at the edge of town. We'll all miss you, Samantha." He turned the knife ominously in his good hand.

"Wait!" Sam grabbed the straps of her pack. "You want the fossil. Maybe we can make a deal." She rummaged in the knapsack and pulled the plaster-covered bone out. "You get the fossil, I get to walk out of here."

His hollow laugh was sinister. "I'll get the fossil anyway – *after* you're dead. That way I'm assured of your silence. You have nothing to bargain with!" He raised the knife and stepped toward her.

Sam stumbled back, bumping into a counter. She'd run out of room and time. Mesmerized, she watched as the shiny blade swung up over the professor's head.

She fumbled behind her hoping for a miracle. Her fingertips grazed something solid. In desperation, she grasped a glass beaker that had been sitting on the counter.

It was as though reality had become a movie where every frame was in stop-motion. The scene played out with excruciating slowness as Sam raised her hand and threw the container. She saw the label on the beaker as it and its contents arced gracefully toward her assailant. *Glacial Acetic Acid.*

The instant the clear liquid touched Professor Caine's face; he dropped the knife and screamed, clutching at his eyes.

The spell was broken. Sam pushed forward past the professor as he clawed at the empty air.

As she slammed the door shut, Sam glimpsed the professor reach the emergency eye-wash station. The water would neutralize the acid, which was only strong vinegar anyway.

As the door closed, she remembered what Jackson had told her about the *Obnoxious Lab*. A giggle, verging on hysteria, bubbled up. The lock on the door was broken and couldn't be opened from the inside. She'd done it! She'd bested him! He was her prisoner now.

Exhausted and near tears, Sam leaned wearily against the wall and collapsed to the floor, still tightly gripping the fossil. "Why are you so valuable? What dusty bone could possibly be worth murder?"

The ragged piece of plaster didn't answer.

The quiet was shattered as Sam heard the lock on the employee entrance click. Her head snapped up. *What now?* With terrifying slowness, the door inched open, and there stood Agent D!

Chapter 18

MYSTERY SOLVED

Muscles frozen, Sam waited, trembling, as Agent D started down the hall toward her. She tried to get up, but her legs were jelly and she couldn't feel her feet. Turning, she crawled toward the far door, praying her security card was where she'd dropped it. Tears blurred her vision.

"Un minuto, señorita Stellar, por favor."

Sam halted her awkward flight. She was done. She couldn't do the whole run, hide, hit or die thing again.

"Sam, wait!" Jackson stood in the door behind Agent D.

Groaning, Sam wondered who else was in on this plot. She struggled to her feet, leaning heavily on the wall as she lurched away. Even though her chances of escape were zero, she couldn't give up.

"Sam, you're not dead!"

This time it was Paige's voice.

Turning, she was surprised to see not only Agent D and Jackson, but Paige, Rose and Doctor Beech. The hallway was positively crowded.

"Thanks for noticing, cousin. What are you all doing here?" she croaked, thoroughly confused.

Paige and Rose pushed past Agent D and Jackson.

"We were so worried, we had to come," Rose explained.

Paige ran to her, squeezing Sam so tightly she couldn't breathe. "Are you all right?"

"I was until you hugged me. What's going on?" Sam wheezed as she pulled away from her cousin.

"It's a long story." Paige moved in for another bear hug.

Sam stepped back. "Can I at least have the condensed version?"

"Right after you tell us where Professor Caine is." Jackson gave her shoulder a gentle squeeze.

Sam indicated the locked Noxious Lab. "He's rinsing his face. There was a little *accident* with some acetic acid. Oh! And his elbow may be broken. You should call for some paramedics when you phone the police."

"Sensible idea, young lady," Doctor Beech said. "I want this matter turned over to the authorities immediately." He left to make the calls.

Sam wanted to laugh. "I never thought I'd be so glad a lock wasn't fixed. That door saved my life." She turned to Paige and Rose. "How did you know to bring reinforcements to my rescue?"

"It all started when I told Jack about the fossil, like we'd planned, Sam," Paige began. "I'd barely told him you had the bone, when things went downhill." She turned to Rose who took up the story from there.

"Paige told Jackson about the fossil and then refused to listen when he said he wasn't the thief and you were in danger. The idea of you in serious trouble scared Paige quite badly, and she became a little…rattled." Rose waited for Jackson to continue.

"By then Rose believed I wasn't the thief and realized how serious the situation was. We both tried unsuccessfully to assure Paige, who was as tight-lipped as a clam. In fact, Sam, you supplied the one piece of evidence that helped convince Paige I was innocent."

Sam was confused. "Me? What evidence?"

He went on. "I figured you were in trouble when Paige told me your plan to turn the fossil over to Dr. Beech. I knew Professor Caine would never let you do that. When I asked her where you were, she wouldn't answer, and when I asked her where the fossil was, she still wouldn't answer. Instead, she started crying."

"I was so scared I couldn't remember the plan so I didn't tell him anything, Sam," Paige piped up proudly.

"About then, I stepped in," Rose interjected. "I told Jackson I didn't know where you'd gone; only that *Operation Dino* was in play."

Jackson continued, "Since Paige was being so uncooperative, I decided to do something to intercept your operation. I searched your room hoping to find the fossil. If Professor Caine came to take it, he'd have to deal with me. I didn't find the fossil. I did find something that helped my case."

Sam waited for him to go on.

"The scrap of paper Professor Caine gave you with his phone numbers on it," Jackson explained. "I showed Paige and she compared that number with the one you'd found in the phone booth. They were the same. Professor Caine was using an office and phone that belonged to another employee who was away which made it confusing. And then I called this gentleman, señor Delgato." He indicated Agent D.

Sam thought of how disappointed she'd been when she'd called the number and found it belonged to Dr. Feldman, the absentee paleontologist.

"He's a policeman with the Colombian government and has been tracking the fossil for months," Paige added excitedly.

Jackson went on. "He explained to Paige how he'd phoned the museum to find out Professor Caine's extension so he could monitor the Professor's calls. What you'd call bugging his phone. It was the phone numbers that finally convinced Paige to let me help. I work with Professor Caine and know all his phone numbers. I wouldn't have had to write them down." He shook his head. "You know, none of this would have happened if my car hadn't been in the repair shop. Señor Delgato came to Calgary earlier than we'd planned, in fact, on the day I was at the university. We decided to ride to Drumheller on the bus, and he would rent a car here. Having him arrive on a Greyhound would certainly keep him under the professor's radar and it gave us a chance to make plans. We figured no one would suspect an innocent tourist visiting the museum."

Sam laughed. "It worked for the Trojans and their big old horse!"

"Oh, Sam," Paige said, her voice cracking. "When Jack started trashing our room, I freaked out. It was a stroke of genius to take the fossil with you. It wasn't until after he showed me the phone numbers and we called Agent D, I mean Mr. Delgato, that I knew he wasn't working with the professor. That's when I told him you'd gone to the museum."

Sam could have kicked herself. "Of course, the phone numbers! I knew they seemed familiar, but I couldn't figure out why. Man, some super spy."

Jackson continued, "You did some excellent deductive reasoning, Sam. I couldn't tell you my early-morning meetings were with señor Delgato and my secrecy made me very suspicious. We were working together to set a trap for Professor Caine; then you dropped into the middle of our plan. When you kept snooping, I tried to head you off any way I could. I thought I'd convinced you to give up on the missing fossil. I have to say, you really had me believing your innocent routine. If you decide not to be a secret agent, you could think about an acting career."

Sam looked from Jackson to señor Delgato, then back to Jackson. "I guess I sort of got in the middle of everyone's plans. Why all the secret stuff? Why didn't Agent D, I mean señor Delgato go to you and ask for the fossil when the shipment arrived?"

Jackson explained, "There was no hard proof Professor Caine was guilty. Señor Delgato had to wait and try to catch him in possession of the fossil. He wasn't sure how the item would be smuggled in or how it would be marked. Finally, the piece showed up and then the darn thing immediately went missing before we could spring the trap. Professor Caine planned on letting things cool down, then he was going to retire from the bone business and leave the museum, taking the fossil with him. From that point on, arresting the professor with the bone became more difficult."

At that moment, the paramedics and police officers arrived with Doctor Beech. Sam watched them enter the Obnoxious Lab, then escort Professor Caine out to the waiting ambulance.

As he was led away, the professor's fierce gaze stabbed into Sam, and her blood froze. Hate radiated from him, and she was very glad Professor Caine was in the custody of the police.

Señor Delgato gave Sam a clipped bow. "Señorita, I am very sorry you were in such grave danger this evening." His moustache twitched. "Although after the way you *fixed* my car in the parking lot, I wasn't sure you would need help."

Sam thought for a moment. "What about the money deposited in Jackson's bank account, and all those hints about leaving?"

Jackson shook his head. "That's the clever part. Professor Caine sent me to South America so I'd be the on the hook for the smuggling. When the Colombian shipment arrived, he took the piece, timing it so I was the probable culprit, and then he electronically deposited the money in my account to throw even more suspicion on me. I unknowingly added to the problem when I mentioned my leaving."

Here he paused. "The reason I may be leaving, and incidentally, my clandestine weekends in Calgary, is that I've been offered a research assistant position at the university. I haven't decided whether or not to take it. I have student loans that would choke a horse and need a boost in my income."

"Have you decided now?" Sam asked.

"I have. Palaeontology is work I love doing and I can't think of anywhere I'd rather do it than here. And I think Doctor Beech is going to need someone to help out on this exotic dino project."

Sam turned to señor Delgato. "Would you mind answering a question?"

"Not at all, señorita."

"If Professor Caine was your man, why were you following me?"

His brow furrowed. "After I heard a fossil was missing from the shipment, I knew Professor Caine had stolen it out from under our noses. When you detected me in the Cretaceous Garden, things became, how do you say, out of control. Then, when he pushed the crates over, I knew we had to get you out of danger and I sent Jackson to chase you off. We knew the fossil was still at the museum, but all our search efforts came up empty. We had no idea you had found it until tonight. "

Sam hefted the plaster-and-burlap-covered fossil. How could something so harmless be worth the trouble it had caused? "I don't understand why anyone would kill for one small bone."

Señor Delgato stepped forward. "If we could go to a work bench, I think I can answer your question, señorita Stellar."

Jackson took them all into the preparation room.

"Watch out." Sam indicated the large bone still suspended from the sling. "Handy things, these dino bones." She patted the unwieldy weapon as they moved past.

Once at a workstation, señor Delgato gave her a chisel and hammer. "Please break the fossil out of its plaster jacket."

Sam took the hammer and gently tapped the chisel against the jacket. The poorly made coating quickly split and fell away revealing a brownish vertebra like all the others Sam had seen. She picked the mystery bone up, holding victory in her palm. "Even when you kept saying it was only a chunk of junk plaster, I knew it was a real fossil, Jackson."

Frowning, Sam hefted the vertebra. "Hey, wait a minute... This weighs hardly anything. This isn't a real fossil at all. It's a cast!" She picked up the hammer. "May I, señor Delgato?"

"By all means, señorita. You've earned it."

Sam laid the cast of the bone on the table and smacked it with the hammer. The cast shattered into a thousand tiny shards.

Sam gasped, so did Paige and Rose. Jackson whistled, while señor Delgato watched knowingly.

There, in the middle of the broken cast, was a large, deep-green stone twinkling up at them. The light reflected from the heart of the crystal and the gem emitted a fiery glow.

"Emerald?" Sam whispered in awe.

"Emerald," señor Delgato confirmed. "Colombia is known for her emeralds, and this," he said, gesturing to the gemstone, "is the biggest and finest quality gem ever discovered in my country. It's worth millions of dollars. Professor Caine and his conspirators stole it over a year ago, and I have been on their trail ever since."

Sam grew thoughtful. "And the other museum thefts provided a perfect smokescreen in case the marked bone was inventoried before it went missing. The loss would have been chalked up to another in the ongoing series of unsolved thefts." Sam shook her head. "Professor Caine is a very clever man."

"*Was* a very clever man, Sam," Jackson corrected. "His days as a mastermind for international jewel heists are over."

Señor Delgato stood at attention. "On behalf of the Colombian government and myself, I want to thank you, *señorita* Sam Stellar. Without you, Professor Caine might very well have escaped."

Sam suddenly felt shy. "It was nothing."

"Nothing!" Paige yelped. "Don't you realize what this means, Sam? It means you actually did some real, honest-to-goodness, secret agent work! All these years we've teased you about your fantasyland, crazy-lady dreams, and now you've gone and done it! James Bond couldn't have solved it any better."

A tingly feeling swept over Sam. Paige was right. She'd been true to her dream and now it was real. "Like Thoreau said – I kept marching to a different drummer. I hoped –" She corrected herself – "I *knew* one day I'd make it as an agent, only I didn't expect it to be so soon."

"I think we should celebrate." Jackson ruffled Sam's hair. "What do you say, Gopher? Are you up for a small party?"

"You bet! Bring on the marching band!" She turned to Rose. "How about you, Rosie? Do you think you could dig up an escort for our little shindig?"

Rose beamed. "I think I know a gentleman to ask the minute we get home."

Jackson bowed to Paige. "Ms Carlson, would you consider being my date?"

Paige's mouth dropped open in a way Sam would expect from a true Jackson Lunde fangirl.

Her hesitation lasted about one millisecond. "Wow! My summer wish has come true. It would be so totally awesome and way cool!" Then, flustered and blushing, Paige added in her most mature voice, "I mean, that would be very nice, Jackson." Everyone laughed and Paige's blush deepened to a furious crimson.

Sam winked at her cousin, then casually scooped up the emerald and gave the precious stone to señor Delgato. "After you've secured this, perhaps you would join our celebration."

"I'd be honoured, señorita."

Sam held her arm straight out, then opened her hand in a mic-drop gesture. "I'd say this wraps up the *Death by Dinosaur Caper*."

She started toward the employee entrance, then stopped and patted her pockets. "Does anyone have a security card? I seem to have dropped mine somewhere!"

If You Dig:
The Royal Tyrrell Museum
of Palaeontology

Location

The Royal Tyrrell Museum is located 6 kilometres from Drumheller, Alberta, Canada. It is situated in the middle of the fossil-bearing strata of the Late Cretaceous Horseshoe Canyon Formation. The specimens contained in the museum have been collected from around the world, but many are from the Alberta badlands, Dinosaur Provincial Park and the Devil's Coulee Dinosaur Egg Site.

Royal Tyrrell Museum, 1500 N Dinosaur Trail, Drumheller, Alberta, Canada.

History

On August 12, 1884, Joseph Burr Tyrrell, a geologist with the Geological Survey of Canada, discovered a seventy-million-year-old carnivorous dinosaur skull near present-day Drumheller. This dinosaur was later named *Albertosaurus sarcophagus* which means Flesh-eating Lizard from Alberta.

On September 25, 1985, the museum opened to the public. In 1990, the museum was given Royal status.

Joseph Burr Tyrrell

About the Museum

The museum boasts more than 47,000 square feet of fascinating exhibits, displays and dioramas. It is home to more than 120,000 individual fossils.

The museum is a world-class research facility and is unique in that it is open to the public. Arranged by geologic era, the exhibits are grouped by age from oldest to newest, culminating in the Ice Age and the rise of mammals.

These exhibits are arranged in a series of chronological galleries spanning 3.9 billion years. The Dinosaur Hall has over forty mounted dinosaur skeletons, including specimens of *Tyrannosaurus rex*, *Albertosaurus*, *Stegosaurus* and *Triceratops*.

The museum boasts its own fossil of a *Tyrannosaurus rex* skull that was named Black Beauty.

Ornithomimus edmontonensis. The skull in the foreground is Black Beauty.

A new gallery, named "Grounds for Discovery," showcases the recently unveiled *Nodosaur, Borealopelta markmitchelli.* There is much more info on this exciting new dinosaur (and gallery) online.

The "Devonian Reef" is a life-size model of a 375-million-year old reef and the "Cretaceous Garden" has representatives of the plants that lived in prehistoric Alberta.

In the "Age of Mammals" we learn about our very distant ancestors.

Through a viewing window, visitors can watch technicians in the "Preparation Lab" prepare fossils for research and exhibition.

Cretaceous Garden

Devonian Reef

Preparation Lab

The Science Hall has interactive stations that introduce visitors to palaeontological concepts, simulated fossil digs, and fossil casting (shown below). It's hands on for the whole family.

There are also guided and self-guided tours of the badlands to enhance the experience for those who really dig dinosaurs.

Seven Wonders of the Badlands Tour

The Royal Tyrrell Museum is dedicated to collecting and presenting the palaeontological history of these long gone plants, animals and eco-systems with special attention to Alberta's incredible fossil history.

Photographs of the museum exhibits and activities are courtesy The Royal Tyrrell Museum of Palaeontology.

If You Dig:
Emeralds

What is an Emerald?

Raw emerald crystals

Cut and polished emerald

Emeralds are gemstones that are green in colour. They belong to the Beryl family and are dug from underground mines. They have a hexagonal shape and a hardness of eight out of ten on the Mohs scale. A diamond, the hardest mineral, has a rating of ten on the Mohs scale which means an emerald is nearly as hard as a diamond. Emeralds are found in several places in the world including Colombia, Zambia and Brazil. The best quality emeralds come from Colombia. Emeralds have also been found in the far north of Canada. The value of the stone depends on its size, colour, purity, and brilliance. The darker the green of the emerald, the more valuable the stone. Emeralds are twenty times rarer than diamonds and are prized for their extraordinary beauty. Scientists have been able to create synthetic emeralds in a laboratory.

Where in the World is Colombia?

Most Colombian emeralds are mined in the eastern portion of the Andes, between the Boyacá and Cundinamarca provinces. There are three major mines in Colombia: Muzo, Coscuez and Chivor which supply most of the countries emeralds.

Colombia, South America

Colombia world map view

History of the Emerald

Emeralds have figured prominently throughout history. The word 'emerald' comes from the ancient Persian word for green gem.

Cleopatra was an Egyptian queen who loved emeralds, and the Roman emperor Nero would watch the gladiator games wearing glasses with emerald lenses.

In the novel *The Wizard of Oz*, by L. Frank Baum, the all-powerful and all-knowing wizard lived in Emerald City, which was made of emeralds.

When the Incas and Aztecs discovered emeralds in Colombia, they became highly valued to these people. The Spanish conquistadors came in the sixteenth century, and when they saw the beauty of this gemstone, they fought for the emerald mines. When the conquistadors returned to Spain, they took the emeralds with them and introduced Europeans to this beautiful gemstone.

The most famous Colombian emeralds are the Devonshire Emerald, the Patricia Emerald and the Crown of the Andes which contains 443 emeralds including the Atahualpa Emerald, named for the last Incan emperor.

Mythology Surrounding the Emerald

There is a Colombian legend that tells of the god Ares who created two immortal beings, a man called Tena and a woman called Fura. Ares told the couple that to remain young and immortal, they must be faithful to each other. When Fura broke this promise, she and Tena became old and died. This saddened Ares and the god took pity on them. Ares changed them into two stone mountains which allowed them to be immortal once again. It is said that Fura cried for all she had lost and her tears became the emeralds found today.

Emeralds are believed to heal the eyes, and one myth states that by looking at them, a person with poor eyesight would have his vision restored. Ancient Egyptians believed emeralds were associated with rebirth and fertility. Many mummies were entombed with emerald necklaces in the hope of bringing eternal youth to the person who had passed away.

It is also believed that emeralds provide protection when traveling and have healing powers. It is said that those who possess emeralds will have good fortune, a better memory, and increased intelligence. This mysterious green gem was also believed to enable the owner to predict the future.

Birthstones, the Zodiac and Celebrations

Emeralds are the birthstone for the month of May and are the gem for the astrological sign of Cancer, June 22 – July 22.

Emeralds are the gift to give for twentieth and thirty-fifth wedding anniversaries.

Photographs in this section are courtesy Wikimedia Commons as follows:
https://commons.wikimedia.org/wiki/File%3AElDoradoEmerald.JPG
https://commons.wikimedia.org/wiki/File%3AEmeraude_Musso.jpg
https://commons.wikimedia.org/wiki/File%3AColombia_Mapa_Oficial.svg
https://commons.wikimedia.org/wiki/File%3AColombia_on_the_globe_
(Colombia_centered).svg

Acknowledgements

It takes a village to write a book, and for this one, I have many to thank:

Mary Blakeslee – friend and support when this all started

Family editors and all round sounding boards – for always being there

John Agnew – publisher for taking a chance

MacKenzie Hamon – for tirelessly working in the background

Maria Alejandra Fleischer – Famous Spanish translator – ole!

Carrie Lunde – Royal Tyrrell Museum of Palaeontology marketing wizard

Amy Kowalchuk – Palaeontology technician extraordinaire

Kathryn Cole – Editor par excellence

Susan Buck – Unstoppable production team

Plus a host of others too numerous to list. To all of you, my sincere and heartfelt thanks.

Author's Note

Death by Dinosaur – A Sam Stellar Mystery, was inspired by my first visit to the Royal Tyrrell Museum of Palaeontology. This murder mystery is a blend of real science and a good old-fashioned who-dunnit.

The Summer Studies and Work Experience program that allows Sam and Paige to work at the Royal Tyrrell Museum of Palaeontology does not exist, (I wish it did!), but the museum does. In fact, the Royal Tyrrell in Drumheller, Alberta, is a museum like no other. It is filled with the most exciting exhibits and fossils any dinosaur enthusiast could dream of. The dioramas and full-scale skeletons will take you back to the time when dinosaurs ruled the earth.

Programs offered include science talks, fossil walks and a camp-in sleepover in the Hall of the Dinosaurs! As the Camp-In information says: *Snore with the dinosaurs, dig for fossils, or create a fossil replica. And then, see what happens when the lights go out at the Museum!*

Overnight Camp-out in the Dinosaur Hall

About the Author

Jacqueline Guest is the author of twenty novels for young readers, many of them award winners, including three previous Coteau Books titles – *The Outcasts of River Falls, The Comic Book War* and *Ghost Messages.*

Nine of Jacqueline's books have been honoured with Canadian Children's Book Centre Our Choice Awards, and in 2012 she won two American Indian Youth Literature Awards. *Ghost Messages* is a Moonbeam Gold Medal winner and a nominee for both the R. Ross Annett Award and the 2012 Silver Birch® Award in the OLA Forest of Reading® program. *Belle of Batoche* was an Ontario Library Association Best Bet Selection and won the Edmonton Schools Best of the Best Award. Jacqueline's books have also received nominations for the Red Cedar, R. Ross Annett, Hackmatack, Golden Eagle, and Arthur Ellis Mystery Awards.

Jacqueline's works are well-known for having main characters who come from different ethnic backgrounds including First Nations, Inuit or Metis. In 2013, she was awarded the Indspire Award in recognition of her outstanding career achievement and in 2017 Jacqueline was awarded the Order of Canada.

Alberta born and raised, Jacqueline Guest lives and writes in a cabin in the pine woods of the Rocky Mountain foothills. Visit her at www.jacquelineguest.com.